FALSE START

CHICAGO ENGINES

GRIDIRON WARRIORS

TL HAMILTON

TL HAMILTON

False Start

Welcome to the Warrior Sports League world.

The authors of the Warrior Sports League have teamed up to bring you professional sports romance stories filled with love, laughter, and heat—on and off the field.

What you need to know:

• While the cities featured are real, the **teams and players are purely fictional**.

• Each book will spotlight teams from across the series, but **they're not part of a single shared season**—so yes, you'll see **multiple champion teams** across different stories.

Get ready to fall for your next favorite player, and don't forget to join the official fan club of the Warrior Sports League on Facebook here: https://www.facebook.com/share/g/9e8NgrPn35epeRDH/

STARTING LINEUP FOR THE GRIDIRON WARRIORS

Annelise Reynolds - San Antonio Rattlers

Heather Dahlgren - New York Nighthawks

KL Donn - Portland Settlers

L.A. Remenicky - Indianapolis Legends

Michelle Savage - Columbus Jaguars

Rachelle Stevensen - Salt Lake City Saints

TL Hamilton - Chicago Engines

Xana Jordan - Colorado Springs Cougars

E.M. Shue - Seattle Westerners

Michelle Rene - Greenville Generals

Cedar Rose - Las Vegas Fortune

Janet Berry - Knoxville Kings

Maria Vickers - St. Louis Mad Dogs

Tarrah Anders - San Francisco Wolves

Haven Rose - Midland Mavericks

Chelle C. Craze - Charleston Crazed Lunatics

Kathleen Kelly - Dakota Dragons

Quinn Ryder - Daytona Devils

SERIES PLAYLIST

GW Playlist: https://bit.ly/3YzMlDg

SCAN ME

Series Playlist:

Annelise Reynolds - Burn It to the Ground by Nickelback

KL Donn - Legend by The Score

Rachelle Stevensen - Here Comes The Boom by Eforce Sub Zero Project

Tarrah Anders - We Ready by Archie Eversole

E.M. Shue - Sabotage by The Bestie Boys

TL Hamilton - Let's Get Ridiculous by Redfoo

Janet Berry - All I Do Is Win by DJ Khaled

Chelle C. Craze - Red Kingdom by Tech N9ne

Kathleen Kelly - Bodies by Drowning Pool

Cedar Rose - Can't Hold Us by Macklemore and Ryan Lewis

L.A.. Remenicky - Welcome to the Jungle by Guns N' Roses

Michelle Rene - Running Down a Dream by Tom Petty

Michelle Savage - Till I Collapse by Eminem

Heather Dahlgren - Light 'Em Up by Fall Out Boy

Quinn Ryder - Crazy Train by Ozzy Osbourne

Haven Rose - Warriors by Imagine Dragons

Maria Vickers - Thunderstruck by AC/DC

Xana Jordan - This is Our House by Bon Jovi

CHAPTER
ONE

Gia

WHY WOULDN'T it sit right?

I glared at the single curl that looped in the wrong direction, making the end stick up as though the whole red mess was giving me the finger.

"Gia. Are you listening?" My agent, Lydia, was a weapon when it came to finding me auditions and opportunities to mingle so I could see and be seen. She was also a ballbuster who didn't understand the anxiety that came with needing to appear perfect.

"You need to move your ass, or you'll be late. Again. Do you really want to keep the casting director for *Shifting Sands* waiting?"

The daytime soap was my dream job. A recurring role that would make me a household name, while hopefully opening the doors to future filming projects. If Tori Redding could go from *Shifting Sands* regular to multi-platinum artist with a movie franchise contract, so could I.

If I wasn't sabotaged by my stupid hair first.

"Who's the casting director?" I asked absently as I sprayed and combed the dark red lock into submission and grabbed my mascara for a final coat.

Makeup and hair products littered my bathroom counter in a chaotic mess that made me itch. *Why couldn't I keep my shit clean?*

Keeping my cell pressed to my ear, I used my other arm to sweep all the products closest to me into the top drawer. I'd hate myself later when I couldn't find anything, but sometimes, out of sight, out of mind, was all that got me through the day.

"Denny Hayes."

At the sound of his name, my messy bathroom ceased to exist as phantom sweaty hands glided over my skin. The rasp of body hair against fabric dug at my skull. My heart thumped hard in my chest, and I grasped the basin in front of me.

"Lydia." My voice came out on a soft plea as I fought the rising memory.

"This is why I didn't tell you. Take a breath, and a Xanax if you have to, but don't let your history get in the way of this opportunity. I convinced him to meet you in public, so instead of getting your panties in a wad, say *thank you Lydia* and get in the damn Uber out front."

Nausea burned my throat, and I swallowed hard as I forced the words out and ended the call. My hands shook with the urge to wipe my face clean and restart my makeup from scratch, to create a perfect mask so no one would see the cracks in my psyche.

Thank god I was one hell of an actress.

Instead of surrendering to the impulse, I gave my

reflection a practiced grin and strode out of my ensuite before I could catalog all the flaws.

The Uber was exactly where Lydia said it would be, and I slid into the backseat with my resting bitch face firmly in place.

"Got a hot date?" the driver asked as he pulled into late afternoon traffic.

God, I hoped the meeting didn't run into dinner time. Dinner led to drinks. Then to hotel invites that couldn't be turned down, if I knew what was good for my career.

Denny Hayes was the kind of creep that made good men hold their daughters a little closer, and I was about to sit across from him and pretend he didn't already take things from me I wasn't willing to give.

"You know, you should smile more. Pretty girl like you."

Shit brown eyes flicked up to me in the rear-view mirror. The look in them was the same thing I'd seen in a hundred other glances from a thousand men who thought they had the right to my time. Taped above the dash was an Illinois state license that told me his name was Donald. Seventy-three years old. A pale band of naked flesh on his left ring finger told me he was recently divorced. My gut told me this was going to be a long-ass ride.

Focus on the goal.

"Are you deaf, sweetheart?" The car swerved as he cast a disapproving glance over his shoulder.

Almost there.

Instead of answering, I focused on tugging my skirt over the small crescent moons my nails left on my thighs, and tried to stop my mind from running through the statistics of women attacked by men in positions of power.

Not an easy feat when I was already one of those statistics.

"Stuck-up bitch," Donald muttered, stopping the car across the road from my destination. He clicked on his hazard lights and flipped off the driver behind us as they expressed their displeasure at his sudden stop.

"Thank you," I said, shuffling across the seats and slipping out onto the road. A horn blared, and I flattened my body against the car as the truck got impatient and pulled around, almost crushing me in the process.

A fine tremor crawled through my body as I finally made it to the front door of the restaurant. I could do this. A quick meeting — hold the food, unless I wanted to vomit all over him — and then back home to safety.

I didn't know if it would be better or worse if he remembered me.

Two large windows broke up the red brick facade of Bar 103, a high-end restaurant that had been making headlines since it opened five years ago. Reservations were a must, unless you were part of the who's who of Chicago high society. Apparently sleazy casting directors were counted amongst the elite.

From the corner of my eye, I caught the shine of one of their gorgeous industrial pendant lights off a bald pate through the window.

My legs seized.

A single bead of sweat rolled down my spine.

Run!

The directive pounded uselessly through my head as the tremors turned into a full body shake. I folded gracelessly to the sidewalk, one hand clawing at my rapidly closing throat.

Fuck, fuck, fuck.

I can't breathe.

The invisible vise around my lungs cranked tighter and sparks danced across my vision.

The revving of cars passing on the street threw me into a deeper memory.

Tail lights glowing on a truck turning out of our street, taking away my chance of escape. Leaving me with her.

Tears burned my eyes, and a whimper worked its way out of my aching throat.

I was alone. A broken doll who had limited use beyond what others took from me.

"Hey. Look at me."

The voice was rough and deep. Commanding in a way that broke through the panic that coursed through my veins. Warm hands cupped my cheeks, encouraging my head up, drawing my eyes away from the slate gray sidewalk to a mammoth of a man crouched in front of me.

I'm dying. I wanted to tell him.

"Breathe with me," he said. His right hand slid down my jaw to loosely collar my throat, while his left brushed over my arm, guiding my fingers to rest on an impressively wide chest.

"Breathe in," he commanded, gently tapping out a beat of four on my fingers.

"And out."

His eyes were hazel with tiny flecks of yellow and green closer to the pupil. I concentrated on the colors as his voice forced me to find my breath and calm the fear hijacking my system.

After what seemed like a lifetime but must have only been a handful of minutes, a shudder passed through my body and my limbs went loose.

"Thank you," I whispered.

"How are you feeling?"

I huffed an exhausted laugh. No way was I about to tell him the truth. It was messy. Inconvenient. No one wanted the real answer to that question.

"I'm fine now, thank you. I'm sorry about that." I forced a smile and drew my legs in, willing my muscles to support me to stand.

A huge hand appeared in front of my face, and the second I slid my palm against his, he hauled me to my feet like I weighed nothing. My knees folded, but he was right there, one hand gripping my hip tightly while I found my balance.

"Do you need me to call you a car or something?"

His lips were set in a tight line. His top lip almost invisible, while the bottom one seemed too full for such a masculine face.

"I'm ok, thank you. I was just heading inside."

Shit. Denny would still be waiting, and the last thing I wanted was to give him an excuse to expect more from the negotiations. Being late to a meeting would make him feel entitled to compensation. A shudder tightened my shoulders, and I took a deliberate step back from my rescuer.

"Actually, I'm late for a meeting. Thank you again for your assistance, but I really need to get inside."

His brow tightened, jaw working like he was chewing on an opinion.

The problem was, I was an opinion magnet when it came to men. Instead of giving him a chance to speak, I brushed past him, reaching for the door. His hand landed on the handle before I got there, and I braced for an insult. A snide remark about owing him for his time.

"Can I know your name?"

The implied request for permission gave me pause. He

wasn't demanding it; he was asking for the right to know. Who the hell was this guy?

"Georgia." Not Gia. Not the persona I used to keep myself sane in the outside world. Even my mom called me Gia, not that that was saying much, but I couldn't overthink the reveal, because through the glass door, Denny Hayes had caught sight of me, and the feeling of his eyes sliding over me was worse than cold, dirty dish water. Reaching deep, I shook off Georgia and became Gia as I left my giant savior at the door and walked into my personal nightmare.

All for the sake of a role.

No wonder they called it a deal with the devil.

CHAPTER
TWO

Gia

THE RESTAURANT FELT like a film set as I strode toward the man who could make or break my career on a whim.

A sea of black tables, polished to a high shine stretched across the floor with blood red chairs tucked in tight. Ringing the room were booths with plush red leather seating for those wanting a little more privacy for their dining experience. Some tables were occupied by well-dressed men and women in business attire, murmuring over glasses of wine and tiny entrées.

I imagined the diners as extras, people strategically placed to fill out the main character's world. The air felt charged, the scents of garlic and tomato mingling with a low-level buzz to create the perfect set for the hero to embark on their journey.

Deep breaths, Starlet, this role is yours.

My favorite podcast, Successfully You, taught me to manifest my goals. "Belief in your achievement is half the battle. Don't talk in terms of I want, or I wish; tell yourself you already have it. Be who you want to become." Athena Colwell, the podcast host's voice, drifted through my mind, and I steeled my spine against the fear of failure, and history repeating, as Denny Hayes rose from a booth at the back of the room and beckoned me closer.

"Gia, so good to see you again."

His veiled reference to our last meeting hung between us as he pulled me into a hug, dropping a kiss on my cheek that left me feeling like a slug had crawled over my body. Instead of letting the memories overcome me like they had outside, I smiled politely as I dropped into the booth across from him and dug my nails into my knees to keep from swiping away the slimy feel of his fish lips from my skin. We were in public. He couldn't do anything in broad daylight with this many witnesses. History would not repeat itself.

Then he slid into the booth beside me.

Don't panic.

I shuffled as far into the corner of the bench as I could, twisting my body to establish space between us.

"This is more cozy, isn't it?" he asked with a pleasant smile. He slid his hand across the gap between us, his fingers brushing against my knee.

"Lydia mentioned you were casting a recurring role for this season of *Shifting Sands*. Thank you for considering me. I'd love to hear about the character," I said, covering a wince as my nail broke the skin on my thigh. The uncomfortable sensation of blood under my nail grounded me as he reached across the table for his tablet.

"Nikkita is an independent contractor who is recruited by Draven to infiltrate Thane's inner circle. She has martial arts training and is an accomplished seductress. There is the potential for a romantic arc and a regular role reprisal if viewers respond favorably to her character's addition to the show."

"That sounds amazing." It did. This role had the diversity to showcase my acting range and, if I did well, had the potential to establish my name in the industry.

"It's a highly sought-after role. You're not the only girl auditioning for this part, but you might be my favorite." Denny's eyes slid over me, full of innuendo. I could tip the casting in my favor if I was willing to give him what he wanted. I had been here before, and the thought of having to live through it again made me want to scream. My talent should speak for itself. I shouldn't have to offer every part of myself unless it was on camera. For a role.

"Sorry I'm late." The voice was vaguely familiar, and it wasn't until I felt a rush of fresh air that I realized someone was addressing our table, and Denny had retreated from me.

"Can I help you?" Denny asked, standing to address a familiar blond giant of a man. It was obvious the move had been intended as a challenge, but the height difference left Denny Hayes looking like a Chihuahua fronting up against a Great Dane.

"Weston Naylor. Pleased to meet you, man. I'm just here to support my girl. Sorry, babe. Parking is a nightmare around here." It was the man from outside. His hazel eyes sparkled with mischief as he leaned close, but didn't touch me.

"You okay?" he asked, his voice a low rumble. A waft of something warm and spicy hit my nose, and I breathed deeply, letting his scent ground me as I dipped my head in a barely there nod.

"Glad you made it." My voice was more breath than

sound, but his lips tipped up in an encouraging smile as he
slid into the seat next to me, forcing Denny back to his side
of the booth.

"Pretend I'm not here," Weston said with a shark-like
grin as he spread his arms along the back of the booth.
From the other side of the table, the move would look like a
claiming. But not a single part of Weston was touching me.
I snorted, covering it quickly as he cast me a curious glance.
The man was a giant. It was a little difficult to ignore his
hulking, yet completely non-threatening vibe.

Well... non-threatening to me.

"I'm confident I would be perfect for this role. You've
seen my work before, and I've continued to expand my
repertoire since then. I have updated headshots and
availability to come to set for screen tests—"

"How long has this been going on?" Denny cut in, his
gaze flicking between me and Weston.

Why did it matter if I had a boyfriend?

"Not long. We'd prefer to keep it low profile for now,"
Weston said smoothly. "Georgie deserves to be recognized
for her talent."

Was he psychic, too?

Wait. Georgie?

I... didn't hate it.

The name was juvenile, and overly familiar, and exactly
what we needed to sell this relationship and the protection
it seemed to provide.

"So it's new," Denny mused, his gaze sliding over to me
once more.

"She made me work for it." Weston sat forward in his
seat, the easiness gone in an instant as he seemed to loom
over the man in front of us.

"When we're ready to announce it, the world will know

we're madly in love and very much exclusive. She's mine. I expect that you will respect our privacy in the meantime. Right?"

The star of my nightmares shrank back in his booth. His knuckles whitened where he gripped the table and despite his submissive posture, something slimy twinkled in the back of his eyes.

"Everyone loves a love story. It would be... advantageous... for Gia to be seen as a public figure when she steps into this role."

When? The word vibrated through me as I sat perfectly still, absorbing this interchange that was simultaneously all about, and had nothing to do with, me.

I had no idea how we'd come to this point. Who the hell was this guy?

Without moving my head, so as not to draw either man's attention, I studied my unexpected ally. His blond hair was pulled up into a messy man bun that was oddly attractive on a man of his build. Usually, I associated the hair style with hipster men in skinny jeans, the kind who cared more about the origin of their daily roast than showering on a schedule.

Weston, however, smelled of fresh laundry sheets and something dark and woodsy. I wanted to lean closer and see if I could sniff out the name of the scent, but that would be a little weird, even if we were pretending to be in love.

"She deserves her privacy." His brows were furrowed, like it truly mattered to him that we controlled the narrative of our relationship.

No shit, Georgia. He doesn't want it getting out that we're faking it.

I mentally face-palmed at my stupidity as Denny let out an unimpressed grunt.

"That's not how show business works."

A woman in the all-black uniform of the Bar 103 waitstaff stepped up to the table and effectively cut off the rising tension between the men.

"Can I get anything for you? Drinks? A menu?"

Denny waved her away without breaking eye contact with Weston.

"Thank you for meeting with me, Miss Kennedy. Mr. Naylor. We'll be in touch about the final casting call by the end of the week."

He heaved out of the booth as I reviewed the last ten minutes in a panicked rush. Had I made any kind of impression with him? Oh god. Had I messed up my chances of getting this role?

I was going to lose my apartment.

Visions swam through my mind of packing up and moving back to Texas. Of having to live under the same roof as my parents again.

I couldn't let that happen.

"Wait!" I called, throwing out a hand and almost slapping an unsuspecting Weston in the face.

Denny Hayes kept walking. With a straight back and rolling stride, he left the restaurant without a backward glance.

"I can't go back to my parents' place," I whimpered, scrubbing my hands over my face in misery.

This was almost worse than how I imagined the day going.

Okay, that was a lie. Submitting to unspeakable things on a casting couch was way worse, but still...

"Do you live with them?" Weston asked, sliding out of the booth and taking the seat Denny had vacated.

"Live with who?"

"Your parents."

"What about them?"

He cocked his head, like he might have been as lost in this conversation as I was.

"You said you had to go back to your parents' place. I was curious if you lived with them. It seems like something a boyfriend should know. Even a fake one." The lift to the corner of his mouth told me he was trying to lighten the situation a little. I didn't blame him after what he witnessed outside.

"I'm not usually that... dramatic. I mean I am, because I'm an actor and it's literally my job — if I ever get cast in anything — but it's not like panic attacks are an everyday occurrence for me. I'm mostly just normal, y'know?"

Weston's lips quivered, like he was fighting off a laugh. Rude. He reached across the table and covered one of my hands with his. The warmth of the move shocked me, and I met his eyes, unsure what was happening.

"Are we having two separate conversations right now?" he asked, giving me a gentle squeeze.

"What...?"

"You don't need to worry about earlier. You clearly have history with that guy, and that's why I couldn't leave you to face him alone. I'm sorry if my jumping in has complicated things for you, but it sounded positive when he left. I'm not sure how any of that relates to your parents, but I'm weirdly curious to find out. Now, can I buy you a drink?"

CHAPTER
THREE

Gia

"So... we're madly in love?" I asked, knocking my shoulder against my new friend's as we spilled out of Bar 103, slightly tipsy and having talked for hours about everything and nothing. I now knew Weston was a closet baker, had the most adorable little neighbor, and had strong opinions on olives and anchovies. We'd steered clear of anything too personal, including work. After Denny Hayes's departure, Weston had considerately avoided any further talk about acting or any future projects. We just enjoyed a night of being in a fake relationship with no strings attached.

The sun sat low on the horizon, painting the Chicago River in a wash of reds and oranges. The breeze lifted the hair on my shoulders and cooled my skin as we wandered along the boardwalk.

Hazel eyes sparkled down at me, a smirk twisting his face into something that had no right to be as attractive as it was on him. It turned out confidence was hot in a man who knew how to stop a panic attack and save an ill-fated interview.

"Desperately."

"And yet I have no idea what you look like naked."

It wasn't until the joke sat in the air between us I realized what I'd suggested. *Stupid drunk brain.* I had trouble controlling my mouth at the best of times, but put a couple of drinks in me and my filter went offline. Weston was hot, and it had been a while since I'd spent any time with a man I liked.

Oh god. He knew it was a joke, right?

Was it?

An endless second stretched beyond my rapidly heating face before Weston threw his head back and barked a laugh.

"All you need to do is ask, Georgie girl. Just ask."

The problem was, now all I could think about was how good it would feel to have his huge hands on me. He had proven he was kind and considerate, but would that translate in the bedroom?

"I mean... it would be a shame to waste this fake date. We can go back to being strangers in the morning, but for tonight..." I let the implication dangle. His eyes darkened, and a responding thrill raced through my body as he closed the space between us.

"A one-night stand to add authenticity to our fake relationship, then back to our own lives tomorrow. Is that what you're proposing, princess?"

A sassy reply sat on the tip of my tongue, but his proximity stole the breath from my lungs. I licked my lips, lifting my chin in agreement.

The smile that broke across his face was both thrilling

and a little terrifying as he swept my hair back and cupped my nape in one large palm.

"Then I should probably start by knowing what you taste like." Keeping his grip gentle, he tilted my head and planted his lips against mine. They were softer than I expected. Pillowy and warm and the perfect pressure as they molded against my own like they belonged there. His other hand slid over my hip and around to the small of my back, and a whimper worked its way up my throat as he pulled me tightly against his firm body.

The moment was wonderful, perfect, and I needed more.

His collar crinkled beneath my fist as I pulled myself up to my tiptoes, licking at his mouth to encourage him to open for me. An amused hum was all the warning I had before he took back control. A sharp tug at my scalp sent a shiver of lust through me as he fisted my hair, plunging his tongue into my mouth in a possessive sweep that weakened my knees and dampened my panties.

More. I needed more.

Smoothing a hand over his wide chest, I vaguely noted the crazy firm muscle underneath before easing down over his abs. This man was going to devastate me in the best way, and the sooner we started, the better it was going to feel. As my fingers brushed his belt buckle, I wanted to cheer, but in the next moment, I was grasping at nothing. Cold air filled the space he'd put between us.

"What...?" My mind was slow coming back online. Lust clogged my mental gears as if my brain was filled with cotton candy.

Weston raked a hand through his hair, the other positioned in front of his crotch as he glanced around at... the very public place we stood in.

Oh.

"If we go any further, we're going to get arrested for public indecency," he said, his flushed face indicating he had been as caught up in the moment as I was.

"I suppose we should probably find somewhere a little less public if we want to get more indecent, then."

Weston breathed out a hard curse, his eyes dancing with something that could have been amusement.

"You're something else, you know that?"

I shrugged. Something about him put me at ease. Maybe it was the fact he'd helped me out today. Maybe that we'd agreed to tonight only.

Either way, I was embracing the time we had. The problem was logistics.

As though he read my mind, Weston fished his cell from his pocket, casting a quick glance at me before clicking away at the screen.

Finally, I'd found a flaw in this beautiful man. He kept the keyboard noises on. I bet he didn't keep his cell constantly on silent, either.

Oh god. Maybe he answered every time it rang, too.

Before I could overwhelm myself with catastrophic phone faux pas, Weston squeezed my hand.

"I have an idea. Give me just a second." He lifted the device to his ear and stepped away.

"Hey, man. Can I ask a favor?"

His conversation was short, and a moment later, he came striding back with a smile.

"My friend has a place nearby we can borrow." He paused, studying my face as though he could read my thoughts through sheer force of will.

"Unless you've changed your mind?"

"Do you keep your cell on silent? Or are you an assigned ringtone kind of guy?"

"Both." His lip twitched.

"How...? You know what? Never mind. Let's go to your friend's sex dungeon." I took the lead back toward the road as Weston doubled over with a coughing fit.

"Jesus," he muttered, catching up to me a moment later.

"Should we get an Uber?"

"No need. It's only two blocks that way. Unless your shoes are hurting?"

I glanced at my feet. The stilettos I'd matched with my dress this morning were my old faithfuls. Cute and worn in, I'd forgotten I was wearing them until he mentioned it.

"I'm fine. Lead the way."

Less than five minutes later, we walked up to a well-appointed apartment building with keycode access. Once inside, we took the elevator to the top floor, and once again, Weston keyed in a code to give us access to the door on the right.

As he hit the lights, a beautiful open floorplan was revealed. Deeply stained wooden floorboards stretched across the expanse of a combination living room/kitchen layout with perfectly placed furniture and tasteful art decorating the walls.

"Can I get you a drink?" he asked as I sank into the butter-soft cream leather sofa.

"Yes, please. Whatever you're having."

I tugged the hem of my dress down over my knees as he retrieved two bottles of beer from the fridge and took a seat beside me.

"This place is beautiful," I said, accepting a drink.

Now that we were alone, the mood had shifted. Slowed.

Maybe he had asked if I was still interested because he had been having second thoughts.

"Do you still want me?"

Weston's head snapped toward me, his brow furrowed like he'd lost the thread of the conversation.

"Yes. Very much so. But only if you're comfortable. What made you think I might not?"

Apparently, I'd misread the situation again.

Stupid Georgia.

"I guess because we've gone backward. From making out back to drinking. It's okay if you're bored now. Just tell me, and I'll go."

The beer bottle was cool in my hand. Condensation made the glass slick as I picked at the edge of the label, unwilling to meet Weston's eye.

A thunk on the table in front of us preceded his hand entering my eyeline long enough to take the beer from my hand. There was a second thunk as my bottle joined his and then there was a whole lot of man in my field of view.

"I was trying to be polite," he murmured, cupping my face and forcing my eyes to meet his.

"You're incredibly beautiful, and I've been hard since we walked through the door. I want nothing more than to learn every inch of your body and fuck you until neither one of us can move, but the reality is that regardless of what we told your acquaintance today, we're strangers. I want you to be comfortable, and a willing participant. Not someone who got themselves into a situation, then felt obligated to follow through with because they'd come this far. You're safe with me, Georgia. If you say stop at any point, I want you to know I will."

"Oh," I whispered, a little overwhelmed by his honesty.

I'd never been told I could say no.

And now that I had permission, I didn't feel the need to use it.

Before I could overthink the situation again, I gripped his knee. "Tell me more about how you want to learn my body?"

His rumbling laugh cut off as he pressed his lips to mine, picking up from where we left off earlier. With a quick shift, he laid me out on the sofa, stretching out above me as he slowly stole my mind with his talented tongue.

He hadn't lied about his erection. It pressed insistently into my lower belly as he moved away from my mouth, pressing warm kisses along my cheekbones and toward my ear.

"Fuck, your skin is so soft. I can't wait to taste every inch of you."

I groaned, tilting my hips in search of friction. My skin hummed everywhere his lips landed as he trailed them down my throat and along the neckline of my dress.

"Can I take this off?" he asked, running a finger under the strap.

"Yesss." I arched my back, giving him access to the zipper, and felt a whole body shiver as his fingers brushed along my overheated skin.

He took his time sliding the fabric down my body as I shifted to help him along. I ached for him in a way I didn't remember wanting anyone before.

"Please," I whispered when he paused at my knees. His brow furrowed slightly, his eyes catching on to something. A row of four red crescents ran along each thigh where I had dug my nails in earlier.

"You hurt yourself."

He brushed a gentle finger across the marks on my left thigh.

"You're focusing on the wrong part of my body, Weston."

I didn't want to talk about anxiety or stressors right now. I didn't want to talk at all. Just feel.

Luckily, I knew a great way to get him back on track. Sliding a hand between my shoulder blades, I released the hooks on my bra and dropped it on the floor. I stretched my arms overhead and gave him my best seductive smile.

"I thought you wanted to taste me."

The growl he released was feral as he ran his hands up over my ribs and dropped his head to my chest, sucking and biting at my breasts until the skin flushed pink under his ministrations. His hips moved against me as he worked, and I shamelessly welcomed the friction, meeting every thrust as we worked ourselves into a frenzy of lust.

"You taste like vanilla." His words were hot against my skin as he dragged his mouth down my ribs, making me squirm when he hit a ticklish patch.

"Like orchids and powdered sugar. Fuck, you're addictive, princess."

He reached the top of my panties and raised a questioning glance toward me.

Would I let him continue?

"Don't you dare stop." My face felt hot enough to burn. Arousal flushed my skin with a rosy glow that made every inch feel like an erogenous zone. I was ready to combust, if only he'd light the match.

He lifted a brow at my tone, a smile curving the side of his mouth as he hooked his fingers in the waistband of my underwear and drew them down at a torturously slow pace.

"I wouldn't dream of it."

His golden hair spilled across the top of my thighs as he settled between my legs, and I wondered idly when he had lost his hair tie. I'd never noticed men's hair one way or another, but as he bent his head and blew gently on my swollen pussy, all I could think of was gripping those gorgeous blonde locks and guiding his mouth to where I needed him.

"Look how pretty this pussy is. So pink and wet and... so ready for me. Do you want my tongue, Georgie girl?"

The whimper that slid from my mouth was unlike any sound I'd ever made. Pure animalistic need.

"Good girl."

He didn't ask for further permission. Didn't press gentle kisses or tease around the edges.

He dove in and consumed me like he hadn't eaten in years. His five o'clock shadow scraped against my intimate flesh as he buried his tongue as deep as he could, sending me into a sensory overload. I gripped his hair in both hands, riding the wave of pleasure his mouth built with every flick of his tongue.

"Please," I said, unsure whether I was begging for a reprieve or for him to give me everything. He hummed, the vibration lighting me up as he slid two fingers inside me.

My orgasm barreled through me, overwhelming in the best possible way as he added a third finger, stretching out the pleasure.

"Holy shit," I breathed as he sat back on his heels grinning like the cat that ate the canary.

It was me. I was the canary.

His erection strained at the front of his pants, and I licked my lips at the sight, imagining taking the opportunity to return the favor.

What did he look like? The imprint suggested he was long. Thick, too. Was he wearing boxers? I wanted to explore him as thoroughly as he had me.

But then, unbidden, came the memory of the last man I'd had sex with.

Why do you think I cheated on you? You're a fucking dead fish in bed. You should be thanking me for staying with you. I wouldn't if you weren't so nice to look at.

I didn't think Pete ever actually liked me. He liked showing me off to others, but he got tired of explaining things to me, and apparently, I wasn't good at anything when it came to sex.

What if Weston decided I was bad at sex too?

I glanced at his face and stopped breathing.

Like he'd been waiting for my attention, he slowly raised the fingers he'd just had inside me to his lips and ran his tongue over them, lollipopping them like they were a sweet treat to be savored.

"Fucking delicious."

It's just one night. You're an actress. You can pretend to be good at sex for one night.

My eyes drifted down his torso and I realized that while I was naked and coming harder than I ever had in my life — self-service orgasms included — Weston was still fully clothed.

First rule of good sex: everyone should be naked.

Sending up a prayer for strength to return quickly to my cum-drunk muscles, I hauled myself upright and reached for Weston's shirt.

"Wasn't the whole purpose of this for me to see you naked? You're holding out on me."

Weston huffed a laugh. Wrapping his fingers gently

around my hand, he reached behind his head and slid his shirt off without bothering with the buttons.

"Holy shit." I couldn't decide which part of his body to focus on as Adonis-level muscles flexed and contracted beneath golden skin with his movements. I didn't know men looked like this outside of Hollywood. His well-defined shoulders shrugged as he worked the button and zipper on his pants, and he glanced at me in question with his thumbs hooked in the waistband.

"If you ask me if I'm ready again, I'm taking matters into my own hands," I said, pointedly eyeing the blond trail of hair that teased at what I wanted to see.

"Yes, ma'am." With a cheeky glint in his eye, he pushed down his pants and boxers in one move and straightened with a foil square in hand which held it out to me.

"Care to do the honors?"

With fingers that shook, I ripped open the package and eyed his... package. It was long and even thicker than I'd thought, with a clear bead of pre-cum forming on his plump crown. Without thinking, I leaned forward and lapped it up before rolling the condom over his length.

"Fuuuck, princess. I want to be inside you so badly, but that mouth is temptation itself."

"Next time," I purred, knowing, and regretting, that it was an empty promise.

"For now, show me what you can do with that thing."

His chuckle ghosted across my skin as he came down over me, positioning himself at my entrance and pushing in in a slow, even stroke that stretched me to my limits.

"Are you okay?" he asked, studying my face for signs of discomfort.

"Perfect. Keep going."

When he was fully seated inside me, he took a moment to let me adjust before starting in on a rolling rhythm that seared through me, lighting up parts that had felt dark for a long time.

Sex had always felt like giving something up. Like the men I had been with took their pleasure and to hell with my wants and needs.

With Weston, he was all about giving. Even as he increased his pace, I felt as though it was all designed for me. My pleasure. My needs. I closed my eyes against an unwanted swell of emotion as a gentle, soul-shattering orgasm swept through me.

As he growled through his own release and we floated together in post orgasmic bliss, I realized how lucky I was that this was a one-time-only deal.

My heart wouldn't survive any longer exposure to this man.

CHAPTER
FOUR

Gia

I WOKE up in my own bed the next morning, my body humming with delightful aches from my time with Weston, my fake boyfriend and knight in shining armor.

As we'd dressed after a third round of mutual orgasms, he'd asked for my number, but I wanted our perfect night to remain just that. Perfect. No complications. No strings. He was kind enough to organize an Uber, and I left him at the door with a goodbye kiss and a thanks for the memories.

I'd never felt better about myself after a sexual encounter. Maybe Pete had been wrong, after all. Weston had been highly complimentary of my skills and, even though I would have loved to try giving him a blow job, I felt like I'd aced the one-night stand.

Go me!

The buzzing of my cell distracted me from my self-congratulations. Where had I left it when I got home? I checked through my bed covers first, then my charging station beside the bed. Nothing. But I did find the earring I'd misplaced the week before. I thought its pair might have been in the bathroom, so I went in search of it, wondering if my luck had finally turned. These earrings had been a gift from my sister, Duckie, when we were teens. We didn't always get along — she was Dad's favorite, and I got stuck with Mom by default — but they reminded me of a time when we weren't practically strangers.

I paused in the doorway of my bathroom. The counter was bare, which meant I'd put everything in a drawer before I left yesterday. Cursing, I dropped the earring beside the sink and began lining up the products I used every day along the counter. When I pulled out my toothbrush, I took the opportunity to brush my teeth and wondered if I should shower while I was in the bathroom. My stomach growled, and I headed out to the kitchen to find a loaf of bread and a jar of peanut butter left out on the counter.

As I retrieved a knife from the drawer, a buzzing started up from the direction of my sofa.

Wedged in between the cushions, was my cell with ten missed calls. Several were from my mom — they could definitely wait until I'd had a coffee or three — but the most recent couple were from Lydia. Could she already have an answer about *Shifting Sands*?

I clicked into her contact and called her back.

"Next time you're going to cause a media storm, could you give me a heads-up first?" she demanded as soon as the call connected.

"What are you talking about?"

I sat on the edge of the sofa, my muscles sending a pleasant, if inconveniently timed, reminder of how I'd spent most of the night. He'd been so sweet. Kind, considerate, and...

"I'm sending you a link. You went viral last night. The sports pages ran with it this morning."

"Why do the sports pages care about me?" I asked, clicking into Lydia's text and finding a video of me and Weston kissing beside the river.

"You're lucky you're pretty," Lydia muttered before taking a deep breath.

"Honey, the man you were spending time with last night. Do you know who he is? Because Denny Hayes was under the impression he was your boyfriend. I let him keep believing that because it's good for your image, but I know for a fact you're not seeing anyone."

I was contractually obliged to let Lydia know almost every aspect of my life. Her job was to craft an employable image for me, and that was difficult to do if she didn't know everything the public, or potential employers, may need to know.

"His name is Weston. I met him recently and he was kind enough to... help me out with my interview with Denny."

"Oh honey..." Lydia's tone was all condescension, and I cringed. I hated it when she spoke to me like this. Like I was a complete imbecile who couldn't function without her.

I hated even more that sometimes that was true.

"I know who Weston Naylor is. Everyone in Chicago does. Except, apparently, you. He's the tight end for the Chicago Engines. He's a big somebody, so at least as fake boyfriends go, you could have chosen a lot worse. I'm going to need you to keep this fake romance going while I negotiate your role on *Shifting Sands*, okay?"

The Chicago Engines. I assumed they were a sports team, but I didn't want Lydia to call me stupid again, so while she talked me through her plans for public appearances, I put our call on speaker and brought up a search engine. Weston's name returned pages and pages of results. From statistics, to injury reports, and gossip columns showing pictures of him with a petite brunette, and more recently, blurred photos of him with me.

"Oh my god," I breathed, scrolling through an article that had been posted two hours before.

Naylor's new mystery woman healing heart and shoulder days before his return to the gridiron. The photo attached to the article was of us standing together on a street corner. His head was tilted back mid-laugh as I grinned up at him. It looked like it had been taken from the opposite corner, and I racked my brain for any memory of a camera, or even someone paying too close attention to us. But there was nothing, because for the hours I'd spent in Weston's company, I hadn't seen anything but him. And that was a terrifying thought.

If Lydia wanted us to keep up the image of a couple in love, I was going to have to find a way to keep my heart separate.

If Weston even agreed to continue the act.

"Gia. Are you even listening to me?"

Nope.

"Of course. Weston is a GWL guy who plays for Chicago, and pretending to date him will be good for my career."

"Okay. Firstly, he's a football player. Not just *a* player, either. He's *the* player to watch going into this season. I'll reach out to his team to coordinate some photo opportunities, but for now, they're holding a training session today that's open to the public. Get down there and look like the doting girlfriend. Leave the rest to me."

She sent a pin for the location of the stadium and ended

the call with a promise to send updates as soon as she'd been in touch with Weston's team.

"This could be very good for your career, Gia. I'm talking visibility that could take you beyond *Shifting Sands*."

I made the appropriate noises as I clicked back into the article of Weston with the petite brunette. Was she going to be a complication in all of this?

Then a worse thought occurred to me.

Did she already hold the title of Weston's girlfriend?

Was I a homewrecker?

With too many questions that the internet couldn't answer for me, I took a quick shower, tried my best to make my face and hair immaculate, and then called an Uber.

CHAPTER
FIVE

Weston

THERE WAS nothing better than the smell of fresh cut grass. I took a deep breath as I jogged out onto the gridiron for the first time in far too long. My body hummed with a level of energy I had no right to, considering I'd spent most of the night learning a woman's body instead of sleeping. Maybe sex did cure all ills because I felt god-level ready for training.

"How was your night?" Christian Morales, our star quarterback and my best friend, asked as he jogged toward me. The question was innocent enough, but his eyes sparkled with mischief.

"The best night I've had in a while, my brother. Thank you for letting me use your crash pad."

He scoffed, waving off my thanks as he glanced at the stands where his personal cheer squad sat in their usual seats.

"No thanks needed. It's not like I've had the

opportunity to use it much lately. Zara keeps me too busy. She looked cute, though."

"Who, Zara?" I asked, adjusting the chin strap on my helmet.

"No, man. The redhead from last night. You know you made the sports pages this morning, right?"

"At least they're talking about something other than my shoulder," I muttered, ignoring the slight twinge as I rolled it out. I'd done the physio time, and I'd been cleared to play. My body was going to get with the program.

Christian laughed. "Sorry, brother. They're talking about that too. You're hot on socials at the moment. If you don't have any endorsement deals, you will soon with the attention you're getting."

What the hell was the media saying about me?

I knew better than to look myself up, but while I'd been enjoying the anonymity of spending time with someone who didn't know me as Weston Naylor, the football player who almost lost everything in a bad tackle last year, the local media had apparently been publicizing my downtime. Exactly what I tried to save Georgia from.

Shit. I hoped she was okay.

When she declined my suggestion to swap numbers the night before, I'd been more disappointed than expected, but a couple hours of sleep had given me some much needed perspective. What we'd had last night was explosive. Fun, hot, and exactly what both of us had needed. We'd allowed ourselves that experience knowing it would end as soon as we left Christian's apartment.

She needed to focus on her stuff, while I needed to focus on getting back into the game. With the way my last relationship fell apart, I couldn't see myself trusting anyone anytime soon. Harmony had taken something vital from me when she left, and I wasn't sure it was something I could ever get back.

"Hey," Christian murmured as our team gathered around Coach Laudner for a pre-training brief.

"It's good to see you putting yourself out there again."

I grunted and turned my focus to Coach's start of season speech.

"HOLY SHIT. I think I let Zara talk me into one too many movie nights over the offseason," Christian panted as we moved toward the locker rooms for showers. He grinned, waving at the stands where his sister, Cami, sat with the troublemaker in question.

"It's not the movie nights, it's the monster milkshakes you keep drinking with her that got you in trouble," I said, stretching out the ache in my shoulder as Christian's ten-year-old daughter raced toward the field.

"They're hard to resist." He shrugged, completely unrepentant.

"Daddy, can I go to Amber's house this afternoon?" Zara was the spitting image of Christian. Her dark eyes framed by long black lashes were especially large — all the better to wrap her father around her little finger. Her long brown hair was tied up in a ponytail with maroon and gold ribbons to represent the Engines, and she bounced around with the kind of energy of a natural athlete.

"Have you asked Amber's mother if it's okay?"

"I texted her as you were finishing up. She's fine having Zara for the afternoon, if you're okay with it. Hey Weston, good to see you back," Cami said, stepping up beside us.

"Thanks, good to be back." I knocked knuckles with her.

"Weston Naylor."

A grin spread across my face as I turned to face the woman I thought I'd never see again.

"Who's that?" Cami asked behind me and was quickly shushed by her brother.

"What brings you here, princess?" I asked, striding across the grass toward her.

"We need to talk."

Her hair was pulled back from her face today, the lengths curling down her back in a fiery waterfall and leaving her long, creamy neck exposed. The memory of her taste called to me as I forced myself to focus on her expertly made-up face and the words she was saying. Talk. Yes, I could talk with her.

"What about?" I asked, aiming for a casual stance, despite the sensation of multiple eyes burning into my back. My team were all like brothers. So close, that sometimes boundaries were blurred, and gossip spread faster than wildfire through the changing rooms.

"Have you..." Her startlingly blue eyes flicked toward the field behind me, proving we were, in fact, the center of everyone's collective attention. She lowered her voice and moved a little closer.

"Have you been online this morning?"

"No, but Christian mentioned we'd made the headlines. I'm sorry, I didn't want to drag you into the circus that is preseason football."

Those eyes softened, and she half lifted her hand, as though she were going to touch me but reconsidered. I wanted her to touch me.

"I don't care about attention. I'm an actor. I just didn't expect this all to get complicated so quickly."

She twisted her hands in front of her, chewing on her lip like there were more words she wanted to say.

"Tell me. I'll help if I can," I said, gripping her hands lightly to still them before she hurt herself.

She ducked her head, and a wave of her vanilla scent hit me as her ponytail slipped over her shoulder. "You may regret offering that."

Giving in to the urge to touch her, I cupped her chin, lifting gently until her eyes met mine.

"Tell me."

Her shoulders dropped at the touch of command I put into my voice. I'd noticed it the night before, and the memory threatened to make the situation in my warmup pants a little NSFW.

She liked to give up control, and the idea of a repeat of the night before was becoming less of a bad idea by the minute.

"My manager wants us to keep up our fake relationship."

I paused, perfectly still despite the urge to pull away from her. She wanted to turn my good deed into a publicity stunt. To use me as a way to get her name out there.

Hadn't I done that already?

She hadn't sought me out because after some downtime she'd come to the conclusion we were really fucking compatible and should definitely see where we could go.

It was about the image.

Just like Harmony.

Although, at least Georgia was being open about it.

"She thinks it could be good for both of us. I guess, you're returning to the field after some time off, so it could distract the media from your injury, and it's already helping with my casting potential. Lydia was going to call your manager this morning, but I didn't want you to find out through him. It seemed... cold? I don't know."

She pulled away, pacing off a couple of steps before returning to me, eyes pleading.

"I'm sorry, I can hear myself talk and I feel like an asshole, but I still need to ask. Would you mind?"

I minded very much, but if Trent had been called, there was no way he wouldn't go for it. Especially with the media attention that we apparently already had. As Denny said: people loved a love story.

But if this was going to happen, we'd need ground rules.

"If we're going to do this, it needs to be purely business," I started, pretending not to be hurt at how quickly she nodded.

"That means last night can't happen again."

"Of course not," she agreed, those hands twisting hard enough to whiten her knuckles. A flash of red crescents carved into her thighs flashed through my mind, and I pushed the image away.

"We'll swap numbers so we can send through information we might need to know about each other, but we'll leave it to management to coordinate public appearances."

I was a little worried she would hurt her neck as she continued to nod along with each new rule I set down, but I kept going, needing to control the narrative we were building.

"My last girlfriend left me when I got injured last season. It hurt my brand, and I lost... a lot. When it's time to end this, I want us to work through the breakup narrative together. No going rogue and fucking up my image to make your own look better."

"I wouldn't do that."

"You're willing to pretend to be my girlfriend for an unspecified amount of time to further your career. Forgive me if I'm a little less than trusting."

I regretted the words instantly. She flinched as they landed, emotional arrows cast from a careless bow. I'd witnessed her have a panic attack less than twenty-four hours earlier, and here I was being an asshole because I got my feelings hurt.

Grow the fuck up, Naylor.

"I'm sorry. I didn't mean that."

"Yes, you did." She pulled her shoulders back, looking me square in the eye. "You're right. You don't know anything about me. I'll do my best to help with that while respecting the boundaries you have laid out. I can't thank you enough for doing this. Truly. Hopefully I can find a way to return the favor."

I grunted. This would be a lot easier if I could stop focusing on how fucking beautiful she was.

"Give me your phone." I waited until she retrieved the device, and again for her to unlock it, then keyed in my number and called myself.

"Now you have my number and I have yours. We'll see what our managers come up with and go from there. Deal?"

"Deal." Her voice was a whisper, and I pretended not to notice the watery sheen to her eyes. I needed space and time to figure out how to be her fake boyfriend without being an asshole or losing more of myself than I could afford to give.

CHAPTER
SIX

Weston

"WESTON! HEY! WESTON! COME OUTSIDE!"

I groaned, hauling myself off the sofa and making my way into the backyard of my townhouse. At the fence, a scruffy blonde head appeared, followed almost immediately by a dark head of hair.

"Yes! I told ya he was home," Amber — owner of the blonde head — crowed to Zara, her Australian accent thick despite having lived in Chicago since she was old enough to walk.

That little detail, along with her and her mother's entire life history, was the first conversation I'd had with her when I moved in three years earlier with a freshly signed contract to play for the Engines and a shoulder that hadn't yet been busted. I knew I was playing on borrowed time going into my fourth season, but I'd be damned if I didn't finish strong. Fuck the law of averages with their 3.3 years of play statistic.

"I knew he was home. He brought me here, remember?" Zara's tone was as dry as her father's as she rolled her eyes at her friend.

"Ohh yeah. Anyway," Amber said, returning her attention to me. "I challenge you to a bakeoff. We made brownies, so you have to make cookies and see if ours are better."

I rubbed a thumb over my lip to cover a smile. When I'd moved to Chicago from Washington, I hadn't just found a new team to play for, I'd found a new family. There wasn't anything I wouldn't do for Amber, or her mom, Marina, who ran a psychology practice out of their front room.

"How are we supposed to compare cookies to brownies? Shouldn't I make brownies too? Even the playing field?"

Amber gasped, placing a dramatic hand on her chest as though I'd mortally offended her.

"What are we going to do with that many brownies? That's just dumb. But if you don't have ingredients for cookies, you can do a cake. We'll give you some stuff, but it'll cost you points."

I shook my head, bemused by her logic.

"Give me thirty minutes, but your mom has to be one of the judges. I'm not getting in trouble for ruining your dinner again," I told her with mock severity.

Turning back toward the house, I began mentally running through my pantry as Amber's "That was one time!" echoed behind me.

As I was rolling cookie dough into balls, my cell chimed with an incoming call. Wiping my hands on the nearest dish towel, I put Trent on speaker.

"Hey man, what's up?" I asked, returning to my cookie dough.

"I should be pissed at you for blowing me off yesterday,

but I had an interesting call this morning. Wanna tell me how you ended up fake-dating a starlet?"

"Yeah... funny story..." I filled him in on the events of the previous day — omitting how we ended the night because it was rude to kiss and tell — and how a moment of chivalry had somehow spiraled into news headlines.

I slid the baking pan into the oven and set a timer, waiting through the silence on the other end of the line as Trent thought through the position I'd put myself in.

"How do you feel about continuing this fake dating thing? It seems like an odd move after Harmony," he said eventually.

I grunted, rinsing off my hands. "I know what I'm in for here. With Harmony the relationship was real. I just didn't realize how much of it hinged on me being Weston the football player instead of Weston the man."

The image of a hospital bed flashed through my mind. I'd been high on painkillers, only hours out of surgery when Harmony visited my bedside to tell me she didn't see us working out long term. The media had been speculating about the end of my career while I sweated on feedback from the surgeon about whether my shoulder would ever regain one hundred percent functionality again. The woman I had been ready to propose to, who had come to every one of my games to cheer me on, apparently only had time for me when I was *someone*.

Last I heard, she had shacked up with some baseball player.

Best of luck to him.

"Okay, so it's only for show. I'm going to be honest here, it won't hurt to have her on your arm at events. Her manager is confident she has a role on some soap opera in the pipeline. She's going to bring attention, and attention — good attention — means sponsorship opportunities. Even if you do manage to see out the season, you need to be realistic. The likelihood of you playing again next year is low. You need to start thinking about the long term. What's next? And it'll be a hell of a lot easier if you have padded your savings with endorsement deals. Especially when last year's deals fell through."

That was a nice way of saying every company I had a contract with jumped ship as soon as my shoulder splintered against the gridiron turf.

Chocolate and cinnamon wafted through my kitchen, and I wiped down my counters as Trent began to spitball events Georgia, or Gia, as he kept calling her, and I could attend to see and be seen.

"Pace clothing has a new season launch next week. We can get you on the guest list and hopefully reopen the door for sponsorship."

"Fuck no. They ripped up my contract before I was stretchered off the field."

"It was business, Weston."

"I don't care. I helped them launch that brand. They were just someone else who wanted to use me."

Shit. Maybe I needed to do some soul searching, because the more I thought about the last twelve months, the more I realized I didn't have that many people in my corner when I was just Weston.

The timer on the oven chimed, reminding me there was at least one person who liked me for me... or for my baking skills, at least.

"Look. I can't make you go, but I think it would be a good soft launch for your relationship. I've seen the photos. She's stunning, and you're in better shape than you were this time last year. Go to the event, even if you're only attending as a fuck you to Pace."

Sometimes I hated him being good at what I paid him for.

"Fine. Send me the details. Now, if there isn't anything else, my cookies are about to burn and I don't want to lose this bake-off."

I pulled the tray out of the oven, leaving it to rest on the counter while I grabbed a drinking glass to shape the soft treats into perfect circles.

"How are you actually holding up?" Trent asked, no longer using his manager voice.

"You've been through a lot in the last twelve months, and I know damn well you're not telling me everything."

Like it was responding for me, a small twinge bit through my shoulder.

"I'm good to go. Looking forward to my best season yet. You don't have to worry about me."

The silence down the line told me better than words that he didn't for a minute buy what I was selling.

"I'll send the details through."

The call cut off just as Amber's holler came from over the fence.

"Judging time!!"

I slid the still warm cookies onto a plate, marveling at how much better my life had been since I moved into this town house. Amber and Marina had become a second family to me. Zara had met Amber when Christian brought her around for my housewarming party and the two had been inseparable ever since. My greatest fear when I injured my shoulder wasn't that I'd never play again.

It was that I'd lose my community. My chosen family.

I shouldn't have worried, though. My loved ones hadn't

abandoned me like the rest of the world. If anything, they held on tighter. Marina had checked in daily in the first weeks, pretending she was helping with housework while asking pointed questions about my mental health like only a therapist would.

Amber decreed that my talents really laid in baking, and thus, the bake-offs had begun.

Christian had offered his spare room, but I couldn't bear subjecting him and Zara to the mood I'd been in during those early days when my professional life was in shambles.

"Are you coming? Or are you chicken?" Amber called.

I stepped outside to a chorus of clucking noises.

"You two are trouble from A to Z," I teased, pointing first at the fair head, then the dark one as they peeked over the fence. As usual, the joke was met with peals of delighted laughter.

"Is your mom there?" I asked, holding up my baked goods in offering.

"I'm here. What did they talk you into this time?" Marina replied.

"Cookies."

"Of course."

I dragged the nearest patio chair to the fence and climbed up, peering over to find two ten-year-olds vibrating with excitement, a Tupperware container grasped between them, as Marina reclined on a daybed nearby.

"One cookie each, girls." She pinned me with a dark look, amusement dancing in her eyes. "If Zara goes home high on sugar, I'm sending Christian to you for answers."

I winced dramatically, grinning at the conspiratorial giggles the girls let out. Christian was an amazing father. He'd raised Zara alone since her mother walked out eight years ago. But his obsession with clean eating was unparalleled.

"You'd sell me out? Just like that?"

Marina pushed out of her chair and stole a cookie for herself.

"In a heartbeat. Now, what's this I hear about you having a new girlfriend and when do I get to meet her?"

CHAPTER
SEVEN

Gia

My HAND SHOOK as I swiped on another coat of mascara.

Should I change my dress?

I'd opted for a forest green sheath dress to compliment my hair, but maybe I should have gone with blue to bring out my eyes. I had to look perfect so I didn't embarrass Weston at this launch. Lydia had sent through the details with advice on what to wear and how to behave at the event, and I'd studied the instructions until the words no longer made sense. If I messed this up, I'd do it publicly. Weston would end our arrangement, and *Shifting Sands* would stay nothing more than a dream job that was forever out of reach.

Breathe.

I glanced at my phone where a red dot announced a notification awaited me.

What if he was cancelling?

The thought had me equal parts terrified and strangely

relieved. The Weston I'd spent the night with a week ago hadn't been present in the texts he'd sent me since we agreed to our arrangement. He'd sent practical notes like confirmation of the time and place we would meet tonight, and tickets for his first game of the season. The lack of warmth, while not surprising, hurt more than I cared to admit. I'd openly proposed I use his fame to further my own career. Nowhere in there had he agreed to be nice to me.

It didn't stop me craving the flash of connection I'd felt with him that night.

Taking a deep, centering breath, I unlocked my phone and found a short text.

> Weston: On my way. Will text when I'm out front. It will look better if we arrive together.

I sent a thumbs up and checked the mirror again for any imperfections.

A buzzing echoed through the small bathroom, and for a moment I wondered if Weston was calling to chat. An unwanted thrill ran through me, extinguished almost as quickly when I checked the screen and the name Mom flashed across it.

"Not today, Lucifer," I muttered, rejecting the call and wandering into my closet to find my shoes. I knew I'd have to talk to her eventually, but my anxiety was high enough without her particular brand of 'rip you down to build myself up' love. I wondered if Duckie felt the same way about her, or whether having Dad as a buffer meant she didn't feel as utterly worthless as I did. My phone buzzed with a notification, and I breathed a sigh of relief when it was Weston's name that appeared.

I slipped the device into my purse, then pulled on my shoes in a rush, worried any delay would upset my date.

The noises of the city crashed over me as I stumbled out the front door of my tiny apartment complex. Car horns, raised voices, the rush of tires over asphalt, all of it built to an overwhelming crescendo that faded into the background as I noticed a towering figure leaning casually against a black SUV. The gray suit fit him like a glove, highlighting the breadth of his shoulders and the trim cut of his waist, even in his relaxed pose. Beneath the double breasted collar, a forest green shirt peeked out — a perfect match to the dress I had chosen. He'd forgone a tie and left a couple of buttons undone at the base of his throat. My stomach warmed at the sight, and I had to send a reminder to my vagina to behave. She wasn't getting a redo with this man. He was doing us a favor. That was all.

A very sexy, unattainable favor.

He glanced up from his phone as I stepped onto the sidewalk in front of him, and I had to swallow past a nervous lump as his eyes took a slow sweep over my body.

Did I look appropriate? Should I write off the entire night and go hide under my blankets upstairs?

"You look beautiful," he said, tucking his phone away as he straightened and opened the car door. "Are you ready to go?" He held a hand out toward me, guiding me into the seat.

"Thank you. And yes, please."

Yes, please?

He jogged around the front and slid into the driver's seat a moment later.

"Have you been to one of these events before?" he asked, merging seamlessly into traffic and heading toward downtown.

"Umm... I catered one once. When I first moved to Chicago. I haven't attended as a guest, though. I'm still working on getting my name out there." I cut myself off as I realized I'd stumbled across the elephant in the room. My name was going to be out there now. Because of him.

"Showbusiness is pretty cutthroat, huh?" he asked, but I couldn't read anything in his tone.

Was it condemning? Or was I just hyperaware of the circumstances we had found ourselves in. How were we going to sell this relationship if I stressed over every interaction we had?

"We should talk about how tonight is going to go," I said, picking at the hem of my dress. The more I thought about the event, the more images of us being called out on the fallacy of our relationship danced through my anxious brain.

"What if people know it's not real?"

Weston slowed the car as we approached a red light and turned in his seat. "No one has any reason to suspect it's fake. We can talk about limits in public, though. I want you to be comfortable. Are you okay with hand holding? Is there anywhere you would be uncomfortable with me touching you?"

"I'm ok with anything."

He frowned, glancing at the still red light before refocusing on me.

"Anything is a very broad term. Would you be comfortable with a kiss?"

I hooked my fingers beneath the hem of my dress and pressed my nails into my thighs.

"Anything is fine, Weston. I'm an actress. Boundaries don't exist for us."

"So I could fuck you in the middle of the red carpet and that would be fine and dandy?"

I pressed my nails in harder. Beside me, he was statue-still, his eyes intent on me despite the green light coloring the interior of the truck.

"Whatever you want."

Weston cursed, throwing himself backward in his chair as he forced the truck into gear and accelerated through the now-yellow traffic light. We drove several blocks in silence before Weston cursed again, shaking his head.

"Everyone has a right to boundaries, princess. The only people who would tell you differently are taking advantage of you. I wouldn't do anything to hurt you."

His jaw was set, his eyes resolutely on the road as he steered us around a corner and over the Chicago River.

"I know," I said, wanting to touch him. To impress upon him how much I meant what I was saying.

"I trust you."

I had met a lot of men in my life. Predators, and protectors, and everything in between. I'd become adept at identifying men like Denny Hayes, who would take more than you were willing to give in the name of career progression. Weston Naylor was not one of those men. I knew that from the moment he ordered me to breathe outside Bar 103.

His face softened, and he flicked a quick glance at me before returning his attention to the road.

"Tell me something about you," I blurted, eager to move away from the vulnerable moment we'd created.

"Like what?"

I thought for a moment. What did I want to know about him?

Everything.

We hadn't shared personal details on the night we shared together because the mystique had been part of the fun — though in retrospect, sharing some very basic details might have been helpful — but in the days since then, I'd become an avid researcher into the life of Weston. Unfortunately, it turned out that apart from a career threatening injury, amazing playing statistics, and a public relationship breakdown, there wasn't much to find.

"If you had one day off to do whatever you wanted, what would you do?"

He drummed his thumbs against the steering wheel, humming in thought as we slowed at another corner and turned away from the water.

"I'd do a sunrise hike — maybe Indiana Dunes, or Starved Rock — then go for breakfast with my buddies. I'd talk them into doing something fun, like a round of paintball, or laser tag, or maybe head out to Lake Michigan and spend the afternoon kayaking or kicking a ball around. Maybe make time for a bake-off with my neighbor and chill at home for the evening. Get the guys around and do a cook out, or something. I dunno, I guess a day off would be spent having fun with people I love. How about you?"

The truth was, if I had a day off, I'd either spend the entire day in bed, binge a podcast, or hyperfixate on a new hobby that I'd half finish and never pick up again. Seeing as it sounded the least depressing, I chose option C.

"Probably learn something new."

"That's cool. What kind of things do you like to learn?"

I hadn't planned for follow-up questions.

Luckily, we reached our destination, and his question was lost in a flurry of handing the car over to the valet and posing for cameras as we entered the event hall. Weston's hand was like a brand against my lower back. Warm. Welcome. Dangerous.

Inside, the walls were plastered with larger-than-life photos of athletes in sportswear wearing smoldering expressions I assumed were supposed to entice the average person to purchase compression shorts and brightly colored tank tops. Across the bottom of each image in obnoxiously big letters was the slogan *Set your own Pace.*

"That's the best they could come up with?" I murmured, eyeing a picture of a beautiful woman with masses of braids cascading over her shoulder wearing a lime green sports bra and matching leggings.

"Amara? What's wrong with her?" Weston asked, his voice guarded.

"What? I'm talking about the slogan. It's lazy. The model is stunning, the clothing sets off her skin beautifully, and then it just says set your own pace. Like, geez. Did someone sleep through their deadline?"

Weston huffed, just the ghost of a laugh as his shoulders relaxed.

"I'm not sure, but they were probably well paid, and if you're lucky you might be able to tell them they suck to their face tonight."

I pulled back from him, unable to tell if he was joking. A server who had been walking close behind me stumbled, barely recovering his tray of drinks as Weston pulled me to safety.

"I can't take you anywhere, can I?" he asked. The move had put us chest to chest, and I wondered if he could feel how hard my heart pounded as I tried to maintain eye contact. He really was a beautiful man, especially with his blond hair loose around his shoulders.

"I'm sorry," I said, sliding a cautious hand up his chest. "I don't want to embarrass you tonight."

He dipped his head closer to me, the scent of warm spice with a hint of... cookies? Or something sweet wafted over me. Why did I feel so safe with this man?

He ran a hand up over my shoulder and loosely collared my throat like he had the first time we met. The move made my knees weak, and his arm tightened around my back as he took my weight.

"Good girl," he muttered, his hazel eyes dropping to my throat. "You won't embarrass me. I'm proud to have you on my arm tonight. Besides, fuck these guys. I genuinely wouldn't care if you offended them. They're all assholes."

I nodded along, pretending my panties weren't growing wetter by the minute as we stood together in our bubble. The crowd moved around us like we were invisible, and I had no problem with that. At all. Especially if he continued to call me a good girl.

"Have you eaten today?" he asked, breaking the spell.

"Wha...? I don't know. I don't think so. Why?"

"You need to eat, Georgie girl. Your hands are shaking. Come on, let's check out the canapes."

We followed the crowd into a large ballroom that was full of people mingling over champagne and finger food. I picked up two flutes from a nearby server and offered one to Weston. In return, he passed me a small piece of toast loaded with tomatoes and basil.

People began to approach us in ones and twos, asking the same questions about Weston's shoulder and his career plans, and I tried to stay inconspicuous at his side. The pretty sidepiece who didn't cause a stir. Every time a new plate of food passed, he interrupted the conversation to retrieve a piece of food and offer it to me until I had to beg off before I exploded. It felt... unusual. Someone taking care of me, even in such a small way. I was used to judgment and competition, but he was different.

And I didn't hate it.

As the night wound down, Weston guided me toward his truck with a hand on the small of my back.

"Our first game of the season is next weekend. Will you come?"

I knew nothing about football, but after having spent the night in his company, I'd accept any excuse to see him again.

"I'd love to."

CHAPTER
EIGHT

Gia

WHAT THE HELL had I gotten myself into?

I looked across a sea of people, broken into sections of red and gold with pockets of the teal and silver of the San Francisco Wolves, the visiting team. The noise of the crowd was overwhelming, and as I stood there feeling overdressed in my skirt and heels, I wondered how Weston would even know I had come.

Lydia had told me my seat was in the field level suite. To get there on time and be ready to be photographed.

A harried security guard pointed me in the right direction, and I picked my way through the crowd to a glass walled room behind the end zone. I'd spent hours the night before reading through the *Football for Dummies* website, hoping to get a basic understanding of the game. Inside, a bar lined the back wall, while two rows of huge, plush seats faced the field. Several seats in the front row were occupied by men, women, and children chattering excitedly as others filtered around them retrieving drinks and plates of food from a buffet table set up against the far wall. I stood awkwardly in the doorway, unsure whether seating was allocated, or if I should wait until everyone else had found their place to slot in somewhere.

The rumble of a throat being cleared startled me, and I shifted aside to make room for a distinguished looking grump of a man who scowled at me as he eased past.

I was so out of my depth.

Somehow, I needed to sell the image of an excited football player's girlfriend when all I wanted to do was sink into a hole and disappear.

"You look a little lost."

I jumped at the sound of the masculine voice, so close to my ear. A tall, thin man — taller than me, but he would still have looked tiny next to Weston — leaned against the wall behind me, far closer than was comfortable. His ball cap sat backward on his head, and his posture screamed confidence as he leaned further into my personal space. "Need someone to watch the game with?"

"Not in this lifetime or the next. Fuck off and find someone else's ass to crawl up. She's taken."

The woman was petite, but built like an athlete with her long, dark hair scraped back in a ponytail. Silver hoops hung from her ears, and her nails were perfectly manicured as she waved away my unwelcome visitor.

"You Georgie?" she asked.

"Gia, yeah," I corrected, unsure whether to treat her as a friend or foe. She took me in with a sweep of her light brown eyes and inclined her head toward the group of people I'd noticed on my way in.

"We're over here. Come sit with us."

She led me over to two women who turned with smiles

as we approached. The blonde nodded in greeting while the other, whose hair was bubblegum pink, practically bounced out of her chair.

"Are you Georgie? Hi! I'm Ridley. It's so nice to meet you, we were wondering if West would let us sit with you. This is Marina behind me, and you've already met Cami. Welcome!"

"Hi." I held my hand up in what I hoped passed for a wave. Ridley seemed like... a lot. But it was nice to feel like someone wanted me to be here. I accepted the seat beside her, and Cami sat beside me.

"Are you all here to support Weston?" I asked.

Ridley tittered, while the other two smiled. "No. Well... I mean, kind of? We all love football anyway, but Cami's twin is Christian Morales."

I started at her blankly.

"The quarterback?"

Nothing.

She waved her hand like she could erase my ignorance.

"Anyway, Cami and I have been coming to Christian's games since college, and Marina is Weston's neighbor. So, I guess she's partially here to support Weston, but mostly so the two hooligans can hang out."

Hooligans? I didn't want to ask and seem more stupid, so I sat back and tried to look like I belonged.

I could do this. Yup. This was me... sitting with women I'd just met, about to watch some football.

For the first time in years, I wished Duckie was here. She loved all kinds of sports, and would happily tell me what the hell the difference was between a wide receiver and a tight end.

Why did so many football terms sound dirty?

"So... is Cami short for anything?" I asked, searching for

a safe conversation. She grunted, keeping her eyes on the field where men in teal and silver were running onto the field.

"Camryn. But never use that name unless you want to be punched in the box so hard Weston will be crying into his lonely hand for the next calendar year while you're out of service."

I blinked.

"Noted. That was oddly specific."

Ridley threw back her head, candy-colored curls bouncing as she laughed. This close, she smelled like candy too. Watermelon jolly ranchers.

"Ignore her," she said, grinning, as she patted my forearm. "Cami's a girl's girl, but violence is always her first answer. It's how she keeps up with her twin."

Cami huffed, sitting straighter as a roar went up outside our box and men in dark red and gold jerseys jogged onto the field. Towering above his team mates, Weston looked like even more of a giant than usual decked out in his pads and wearing obscenely tight pants. His ass looked good enough to bite.

"I don't need to keep up with him. If he pisses me off, I just nail him in the balls and leave him to cry into his groupies ample—heeey girls. Where did you run off to?"

Two tiny humans popped up behind our seats with hands full of pastries they'd liberated from the buffet.

So these must be the hooligans.

"Can I nail someone in the balls?" the darker haired of the two asked. She looked a lot like Cami, but I didn't get a mother/daughter vibe.

"Definitely, but only if they deserve it, and you don't tell your father I gave you permission."

"Deal."

"No deal," Marina interrupted, dividing a glare between the two girls. I couldn't place her accent, though she sounded a lot like Margot Robbie when I saw her press tour for the *Barbie* movie. I wanted to ask, but after Cami's threat, I decided it might be safer to just observe for now. They all seemed to be super tight and I didn't want to offend them. I'd never really had girlfriends before, but maybe I could change that with these women.

"Game's starting," Cami announced, and everyone settled in to watch.

"Holy shit!" I screamed, as Weston threw himself at the tank of a San Francisco player who had been barreling toward Cami's brother. The men went down hard in a tangle of limbs, and I jumped to my feet, breath caught in my throat as I waited for him to get up off the ground.

Weston's block cleared the way for Christian's throw, and a moment later a player wearing Chicago colors came hurtling down the grass toward us. A few steps shy of the end zone, the wide receiver for the Engines launched himself through the air and caught the ball one handed, evading the grasp of two San Francisco players as he landed across the line.

"Touchdown!!" The cry was echoed by half the room as people slapped each other on the back and cheered like they'd been the ones who scored.

"That was... exciting," I said, covering my pounding heart as a new player ran onto the field to join the line up of players that felt close enough to touch. On the Chicago side line, I caught a glimpse of Weston's face, pulled into a scowl of concentration that made him look sexy and foreign all at once. He pulled his helmet off, running his fingers through sweat soaked hair, and I felt a pulse of heat run through me.

"I think I like football," I murmured to myself, causing Ridley to laugh again as the ball was snapped and kicked through the goal post. Another cheer rolled around the stadium as red and gold flags waved in the crowd.

The game was thrilling to watch, with the Wolves meeting every touchdown from Chicago with one of their own. Cami and the girls tried to explain the rules as we watched, patiently talking through the nuances of the offensive vs. defensive side, and the skill Christian demonstrated leading the offense.

Not once did they make me feel stupid for my questions, and by the end of the fourth quarter, I felt like I'd found a place where I fit. The Engines won the game, a field goal pushing them into the lead with only minutes left in the game, and Ridley invited me down to the locker rooms with them.

"Weston will want to see you, and we're heading down there anyway."

We fought through the crowds, winding our way through the bowels of the stadium until we reached security personnel outside a set of double doors. Cami approached them with confidence, and after a short exchange, we were waved through.

"In here," Cami's niece, Zara announced, darting through a side door with Amber hot on her heels.

"This is the family and friends room," Marina explained, waving me inside. "There's always fresh snacks." Sure enough, the two girls had already retrieved a can of soda each and commandeered a plate of cookies.

"Zara, if you put yourself in a sugar coma, your dad is

going to lose his mind. Take one and put the rest back. Amber, you've had enough, too."

Marina's mom voice was a little scary.

The girls returned the plate they'd stolen and sat in one of the plush sofas that filled the room.

"The guys will shower and anyone who doesn't have to speak to the press can come in and visit once they're ready," Cami said, finding her own seat.

A pang of disappointment hit me. Weston had looked so fierce and rugged all covered in sweat and dirt. It seemed a shame to wash it all away.

Don't forget, this whole thing is fake. Dirty men don't play into the pretty relationship picture.

I needed to keep my eye on the prize. Lydia hadn't heard back about *Shifting Sands* yet, and if I didn't get the role, relationship or no, my next step would be moving back to Texas.

Living under the same roof as my mother again was not an option.

A loud bang shook me from my miserable thoughts. In the wide-open doorway stood Weston. Sweat glistened on his forehead, his blond hair a riotous mess around his face and neck. His knees were stained with dirt and grass, and his smile was the kind of bright that destroyed a woman's panties right along with her logical mind. Without a thought for appearances, or the lecture I'd just given myself, I took three running steps and jumped into his arms. The adrenaline of the game, the rugged beauty of his appearance, and the feeling of belonging all crawled beneath my skin in a symphony of excitement that I couldn't contain.

"Hey—" I cut him off with my lips and tried to pour all my appreciation and gratitude into the action. Wolf whistles and catcalls rose from the group of women behind us, and I grinned against his mouth as he squeezed me tighter.

"Get a room," Cami called as Amber and Zara broke into fits of giggles.

His lips tasted of salt, the ghost of a beard rough against my cheek, and I didn't want it to end. But the reminder of an audience was enough to make me pull back.

"Hi," I said, squirming in a bid to get him to let me down. He did, though one hand stayed wrapped in my hair while the other rested on my hip.

"Did you enjoy the game?" he asked.

I nodded, licking my lips as my eyes dropped to his mouth again. It was the closest we'd been since the night we spent together. Technically, I'd broken the rules of our deal, but I couldn't find it in me to care. Especially as my libido tried to convince me we should do a repeat on the whole experience.

"Princess..."

I glanced up at him as his words died out. Hunger. Everything I felt was right there, reflected in his eyes, and I wondered how much of this arrangement was actually fake.

"Okay, we got some good shots of the two of you. Mr. Naylor, are you doing the press conference?" A man in jeans and button up shirt broke in on the moment with an old school camera looped around his neck.

I took a step back and wrapped my arms around my middle as he stole Weston's attention. Had I unknowingly played into a publicity stunt? Of course I had. Weston had made it clear that he would help out with the fake relationship, but that he didn't want anything more.

I hadn't even realized the guy was in the room.

With a deep breath, I pulled on my acting skills and projected the persona of a confident girlfriend to the people gathered in the room.

No one needed to know I'd already gotten lost in the moment.

Least of all Weston.

CHAPTER
NINE

Weston

WE FINISHED off the preseason with a punishing away game that put us in a good place going into the regular season, but left me bruised and wishing that the week would drag before our next game.

The early morning Chicago air lifted my hair as I locked up my car and headed toward the shores of 12th Street beach. Trent had called me about a sponsorship opportunity that had come as a result of the photos of Georgia and me after our first preseason game.

I'd accepted because the offer was from Elite Mind clothing — Pace's biggest competitors. The premise of the shoot was *supporting your goals*.

There was also the added bonus of the other model for the shoot...

"Morning." Her voice was sweet and husky like she'd only just woken up. Georgia's hair was a mass of unruly curls on top of her head, and I did a double take as I realized she wasn't wearing makeup. She looked younger. Vulnerable, somehow without the usual immaculate shades she painted her face in. I liked her like this. And wasn't that a dangerous thought for a whole lot of reasons.

"How did you sleep?" she asked as we made our way down the sand to a tent that had been set up for hair, makeup, and wardrobe changes.

"Fine. You?"

No reason for her to know my subconscious had taken to replaying the highlights of our night together on repeat every time I closed my eyes. The sounds she made, the taste of her on my tongue, her smooth skin beneath my fingers. All of it came together to ensure that while I wasn't losing sleep, I could possibly end up losing my mind over this woman. The lines felt blurred already, and I hadn't helped the situation by giving in to the urge to take care of things in the shower before I left home.

"Good." The rushing of the waves on the shore only served to amplify the awkward silence that sprang up between us as a small woman stepped out of the tent.

"You must be Weston and Gia. Come in. I'm Vera, I'll be your photographer today." She ushered us into the dimly lit space and pointed out two chairs.

"Aren't you two just gorgeous. Sit tight and the makeup artist and hairdresser will be in in a moment to get you sorted. We're starting with the athleisure wear, then the lounge wear, then we'll finish with the sports range after sunrise. How does that sound?"

I had no idea how Vera had so much energy at this time of the morning, but it was shared by the artists who came in and made me presentable while turning Georgia into a goddess.

For the next few hours, I was put through a special kind

of torture as we wore outfit after outfit and moved through close, intimate poses all in the name of selling clothing. Unfortunately, my libido didn't get the memo we were trying to be professional. Every time I caught a whiff of her vanilla scent, or ran my hand over her skin, fireworks exploded in my nervous system, insisting we should find somewhere a little more private.

We wrapped up shooting as the sky shifted from the pinks and oranges of sunrise into the blue of a stunning late summer day.

"Can I take you to breakfast?" I asked Georgia as we arrived back at our cars.

"I'd like that," she said and pressed the button on her fob. Her car unlocked with a loud thunk and flashing headlights. "Where should we go?"

I wanted to take her home. To show her how good I was in the kitchen. And other places. But our goal was publicity, and we couldn't be photographed there. Instead, I suggested a local favorite, where the pancakes were stacked high and fluffy, and the coffee was bottomless. She agreed easily and slipped into the driver's seat of her car, promising to meet me there.

Traffic was light as I followed her through the urban streets. A couple of cars passed, filled with children on their way to weekend sports by the look of the matching jerseys. A lone pedestrian jogged along the sidewalk as a group of cyclists passed on the opposite side of the street. Even in the stillness, there was a life to the city.

I pulled into the parking spot beside Georgia's and met her at the door to the diner, holding it open to let her through first before trailing inside.

"Sit anywhere you like." The woman behind the counter had a kind, weathered face, and she spared us a smile as we entered before turning her attention back to the newspaper in front of her. "I'll be with you in a minute."

I rubbed at my shoulder as we took our seats and Georgia gave me a curious look. A dull ache had been throbbing through the joint since I woke up, but there was no way I would acknowledge it out loud. I'd pull out my physio bands when I got home and do some work on it instead.

"Have you heard anything about your show yet?" I asked.

She shook her head, squaring the edge of her menu along the side of the table.

"Not yet. Lydia has a meeting this morning, so I should find out today. I don't know what I'll do if I don't get it."

"You'll get it," I said with absolute confidence. She was stunning, talented, and interesting to be around. I found it hard to believe the casting directors wouldn't see what an asset she'd be to the show.

"There are a lot of people trying for the role. I was lucky to get as far as I did. I just don't want all this to have been for nothing."

Because it was such a chore to spend time with me.

Stop being a whiny bitch.

I'd never met a woman as hard to read as Georgia, and maybe that was the truest testament to her acting skills because I kept forgetting we were pretending. When we were together, I felt like she was mine. Like maybe she was worth the risk. But every time reality came crashing in to remind me I didn't get that. I had my shot and broke it as effectively as I did my shoulder.

With a tight-lipped smile, I turned my attention to the menu, studying the options like they held the answer to life's mysteries.

"Thank you for everything you've done for me, Weston. I don't feel like I can say that enough. You're... so much more than I ever expected."

"Let's just hope you get that call soon."

We fell silent until the waitress brought over coffee and took our orders. I breathed deeply, appreciating the smells of butter and bacon, with a bitter undernote of coffee filling the air. Georgia fidgeted with her menu. The salt and pepper shakers. She bounced her knee under the table.

I was being belligerent and making her nervous. My own hang-ups weren't her fault.

"So where are you from? That first night you spoke about moving back in with your parents. Where are they?"

The new subject didn't seem to make her any more comfortable, but she told me a little about growing up in Texas with her sister. About how Duckie was the tomboy and their father's favorite. About how their mother had pushed Georgia to more traditionally feminine things. Her posture caved in on itself as she spoke about the woman who birthed her, and I took the first opportunity to redirect the conversation.

"Duckie is an interesting name."

She snorted. "Her real name is Blair, but she's had the nickname since we were teens. I can't remember who came up with it."

"So Blair lives in Texas still?"

She flashed me a surprisingly dark look over her coffee cup as she took a long sip.

"Yeah, she does. You'd probably get along well with her. She works for the hockey team down there. She doesn't look like me, though. She's the smart one."

"I think you're smart."

Georgia brought her mug down on the table a little too

hard and coffee spilled across her laminated menu. With a curse, she pulled a handful of napkins out of the silver holder and roughly swiped at the mess.

"Hey," I said and froze as she flicked watery eyes up toward me before refocusing on the mess in front of her.

"I don't need you to patronize me, Weston. I know what I am and what I'm not. Trust me. I've spent my life surrounded by people who were all too happy to fill me in on my shortcomings. I'm pretty. That's it. Nothing below the surface. My life will be done at the first sign of wrinkles, and I'm already on the wrong side of twenty-five."

She scrubbed her hands over her thighs, avoiding eye contact as I processed her outburst. It was obvious she meant every word, but what I couldn't come to terms with was the fact she didn't have anyone in her corner to refute the beliefs. Until now.

"It sounds like you've been surrounded by the wrong kinds of people for a long time," I said carefully, trying to catch her eye.

I could fix this. I wasn't sure how yet, but there had to be a way to help her. Even if she was using me for the clout, everyone deserved to have people at their back.

The answer came to me in a nauseating wave of vulnerability.

"When I injured my shoulder last year, I thought that was it for me," I said.

Now it was my turn to take an interest in the dishes as her head shot up. I wrapped my hands around my empty mug and knocked it gently against the table as I thought through my words.

"I told you my girlfriend left me when I got injured. She didn't want the washed-up has-been she thought I'd become. I learned who my true friends were during that time. People who would always have my back, like family. Well, like family should," I corrected as she flinched.

"I promise, no matter what happens between us, I'll be honest with you, and I'll have your back."

A tear splashed on the table in front of her, and she swiped at her eyes.

"You don't have to do that," she said.

I reached across the table and squeezed her wrist. Beneath my fingers, I could feel her trembling.

"I want to. You and me? We're in this together."

Her eyes were glassy as she held my gaze, but beneath the tears there was a spark of hope that I wanted to fan. To build into a blazing inferno of confidence in the amazing woman I knew she could be without people tearing her down at every turn.

"You're too good to me," she said, the corner of her mouth turning up.

From the corner of my eye, I caught the waitress approaching with our food, so with a final squeeze, I sat back and accepted my plate.

"We'll be good to each other," I said, smiling at her nod.

With our cards on the table, we ate in a companionable silence until her phone started rattling across the table.

"I'm sorry, it's Lydia. Do you mind if I take this?"

I waved her on and she answered with a tense *hello*.

The conversation was mostly one sided with Georgia giving an occasional "uh huh" and "really?"

Her face told the real story. Tension gave way to concern, then confusion, cautious optimism, followed by a breathtaking smile as she thanked her manager and ended the call.

"Good news?"

"I got it." Her face shone as she half stood, then sat,

wriggling around in her chair like she wasn't sure what to do with herself.

"I got the role! I'm going to be on *Shifting Sands!*"

I'd never seen the show, but it wasn't for me to decide how exciting the news was. She'd worked her ass off for the role, so there was only one response necessary.

"Congratulations!"

She burst out of her seat and rounded the table, and I was right there to catch her as she threw herself into my arms. Her enthusiasm was infectious and, without thought, I pulled her into a kiss. Her body immediately molded to mine as I licked my way into her mouth. Her taste exploded on my tastebuds, and I groaned at the pinch of her nails biting into my chest.

"Well done, princess. You deserve it," I muttered against her lips. She hummed, pressing closer to me.

"Don't forget we're in public, Georgie girl."

She huffed, breaking the kiss. "Are you reminding me? Or yourself?" she asked as she deliberately brushed her hip against my erection. I hissed at the contact and slipped back onto my chair as she sashayed back to her seat.

"We need to celebrate."

"Isn't this a celebration?" she asked, then a dark smile lit her face. "Or do you mean something a little more intimate?"

I groaned at her implication and sent a harsh command to my dick to behave.

"I thought maybe we could have a cookout at my place. Maybe invite a few friends over to celebrate the fact you're a badass actor who will be the best thing to ever happen to that TV show."

She hummed, her eyes focused on the table in front of her.

"I don't really know who to invite."

"What about Cami? Marina? Ridley?"

"Why would they care that I got the role?"

"Georgie, they like you. They'd be happy for you because you're happy. That's what friends do."

She gave me a dubious look, but shrugged.

"If you want. It could be fun."

If I did nothing else in this fake relationship, I was going to teach this woman that she was worth something to people.

Even if it cost me everything.

CHAPTER
TEN

Gia

AFTER BREAKFAST, Weston headed to the gym while I went home to prepare for a night of socializing. I ignored another call from my mother, and at six-thirty, my alarm went off to remind me it was time to head to Weston's house. The trouble was that I'd decided to repaint my bedroom wall. The plum color was beautiful against the cream trimmings, and I had finished cutting in the final corner when the alarm blared from beneath the pile of my bedroom furnishings I'd made in the middle of the room.

I cursed, wiping my hands on a scrap of fabric as I hunted through clothing and knickknacks to find the device. Silencing it with a jab, I caught my reflection in the mirror above my bureau. My face and neck streaked in paint.

Why was I like this?

I rushed through a shower and reapplied my makeup, acutely aware of time ticking away. Weston had offered to host a celebration for me, and I couldn't even have my shit together enough to be on time. With a final spritz of my favorite perfume, I rushed down to my car and keyed his address into my navigation system. The upside of him living in the suburbs was parking would be easy and traffic light. I used Ubers when I had to get around the city because the cost was worth avoiding driving and parking anxiety.

As I was putting the car in reverse, a text from Weston popped up on my phone.

> Weston: We're all set up. Looking forward to seeing you soon.

I responded with a heart and focused on getting myself there in one piece.

When I arrived at the address, I was surprised to find a row of townhouses. Beautiful two-storied homes that looked like they cost more than my car for a week's rent. Never mind how much they must cost to own.

As I locked up and stepped onto the curb, the reality of the gap between where Weston belonged and where I was felt insurmountable. I'd known I was using him to further my career, but this all made me wonder why he was playing along. Whatever feelings I'd been growing toward the man who had so thoughtfully decided to help me celebrate my milestone had to be put down. He was well out of my league.

"Hey, did you just get here?" Marina stepped out of the house next door with a friendly smile.

"Ah…" I looked back at my car, then at the house. "Yeah. I lost track of time." The smile I gave her felt plastic, but she returned it with genuine warmth as she stepped in and gave me a brief hug. "Congratulations.

West let slip that you got the role. You must be so excited."

"It's a dream come true."

"It sounds like you earned it," she said, ushering me up the walk and through the front door. The open concept layout was gorgeous, from the comfortable looking lounge area at the front, to the giant kitchen that looked like something Martha Stewart would have been happy preparing food in.

"This is…wow."

Marina snorted, retrieving a bottle of white wine from the fridge. "I know. One hell of a bachelor pad, right?"

"There you are." Weston stepped through the back door wearing a grin and a black apron.

"Help yourself to anything in the kitchen and come outside. Everyone's excited to see you."

I hesitated at the word everyone. When he said he'd invite a few friends, I hadn't clarified. It could have just been the people I knew, or the entire football team. I didn't feel like I had the right to decide who Weston invited into his house.

Marina offered me a glass of wine, and I accepted it eagerly before trailing after her onto the back patio where an outdoor dining area was decorated with strings of fairy lights, giving it a magical vibe. The only other man present was Christian, and the seats around the table were taken up by Cami and Ridley as Marina made space for me to sit with them.

"The woman of the hour!" Ridley crowed.

Heat crept up my throat at their attention, but I managed a small bow before I sat.

It turned out that Ridley had been a fan of *Shifting Sands* when she was younger, but she still kept up with the storylines from time to time. They all seemed impressed that a strong female character was being introduced, and even more so when they found out I would be training to do my own stunts.

"That's amazing! You should come to the gym with me some time," Cami said, waving off the others as they shouted warnings.

Cami was a pitcher in a women's baseball league and held just about every record a female pitcher could. Her next career move was to go into coaching.

"That sounds really cool. Do you have a team planned?" I asked, happy to share the limelight.

"Not yet. I'm talking with a couple of teams, but it'd be nice to stay in Chicago." Around the table, everyone made sounds of agreement, and I took a deep breath as that feeling of belonging hit me again.

The smells of cooking meat and caramelized sugar made my mouth water, and I glanced toward Weston who stood by the grill chatting with Christian.

Like he could sense my eyes on him, he glanced my way and smiled.

I was in so much trouble.

"You guys are good for each other," Marina murmured.

Ridley and Cami continued with their conversation, but Marina's eyes were firm on me.

"I don't know how good I am for him."

She made a rude noise. "You didn't see him last year. Honestly, we've been worried about him for a while, but he seems better since he met you. Happier. It's really nice to see."

Guilt stabbed through me at the lie we were keeping. Would they think the same thing if they knew I was using him? Even with his permission, I felt like a shitty human being.

It occurred to me that when this all ended, I'd lose these people too. Not just Weston, but all of them.

Marina's words stayed with me through dinner and dessert, where Weston proved that he hadn't exaggerated his baking prowess with an assortment of pastries that admittedly turned me on a little more than they should have.

Why were sweets hot?

Marina and Christian made their excuses first, keen to check in on the sleepover the girls were having next door. "They were pitching a scary movie before we left, and if they decided to watch it despite what we said, it's going to be a long night," Marina said with a rueful shake of her head. Christian chuckled, but his brows pinched like he might have been equally worried for his sleep.

Each of them gave me one last congratulations, then headed out.

Cami and Ridley didn't last much longer before heading home.

"I can stay and help with clean up," I murmured to Weston as we waved them off at the door.

"Thank you," he said, closing the door behind us as I went in search of garbage bags.

"It's the least I could do. Thank you for tonight, it meant a lot." I poked my head into cupboards as I spoke, unsure what kind of sorting system he had set up, and wanting to downplay how much his gesture had really meant to me.

He leaned a hip against the counter and pointed to a cupboard beneath the sink. "Bags are in there. Could you pass me a second one for recycling?"

We worked together efficiently, clearing the bottles and debris of the celebration in companionable silence. Once it was cleared, we settled on two loungers at the edge of his outdoor space.

"How is it that when I'm with you I don't feel the need to be anyone but myself?" I pondered aloud.

"I'll take that as a compliment." His voice was warm with a hint of amusement.

"I'm serious." I rolled to my side to look him in the eye. "It's like... I'm safe to drop the mask. It's fucking terrifying."

Weston pulled himself upright, sitting on the edge of his lounge chair. "Why is it terrifying?"

"Because it's going to end."

He rubbed his hands together, head bowed, as the sounds of the night filled the silent backyard.

"You have the job now," he said after a while. It felt far too close to a goodbye for my liking.

"I don't think we should stop just yet, though. You said it should be mutual, and if we break up as soon as I get the role, it'll look like I used you."

Never mind that I did. That despite what Marina said, I was very much the only one benefiting from this arrangement. I couldn't let it end yet.

"So we continue," he said, studying me. I mostly hid my sigh of relief as I nodded. "Until it's safe to stop."

I didn't mention my growing wish that that day would never come.

My body felt warm. Full of good food, good wine, and maybe a little more than like for the man beside me.

The desire to give him pleasure had only grown since our night together, and with the thoughtful gathering he'd arranged just for me, there was only one way I wanted to show my appreciation.

"I've been thinking about something."

Weston cocked his head, waiting for me to continue.

"I want to say thank you for tonight, and I believe there's an IOU owing. Lie back."

Without further instruction, he shuffled around and stretched out, hooking an arm behind his head as he watched me through heavy lids.

"You don't owe me anything, for the record."

"I do. But I also really, really want to." I slid to my knees beside his chair and reached for the waistband on his jeans, opening them with quick fingers to free his growing erection. I licked my lips at the sight, already keen for the taste of him on my tongue as he growled low in his throat.

"You look hungry, princess. What do you want?"

"This." I ran my fist up and over his length, squeezing at the tip before I angled it toward my lips.

"Fuck yes," he growled as I flattened my tongue and ran it over his head, savoring the bitter taste of pre-cum before I took him to the back of my throat, experimenting with depth and humming as his excitement warmed my own blood. He speared a hand through my hair, keeping his view clear as I worked over him enthusiastically.

"You take me so well, princess. This mouth was made for me. Can you squeeze a little tighter?" I followed the instruction, tightening my fist at the base of his cock and was rewarded with a filthy groan that went straight to my clit. Unable to stand the ache, I slid a hand into my panties as Weston's sounds grew more urgent.

"Are you touching yourself? Don't come yet, I want to watch you fuck yourself to orgasm after you swallow me down. Can you wait for me?"

I whimpered, nodding as I tried to slow down. I wanted to be good for him.

"Baby, I'm not going to last much longer. You feel so fucking good, are you ready for me to finish?"

A shiver ran through me, and I took him as deep as I could, twisting my saliva-covered fist at his base as his entire body tightened.

"Fuck, yes princess," he barked as I swallowed fast against the flood of cum pouring down my throat.

"Such a good girl. Take all of me." He stroked my hair, my throat, all the while cooing words of affection that turned me into a puddle of need. When the last shudder left his body, he turned dark eyes on me. "Take off your skirt and panties, and lie back on your chair."

I followed his direction, ignoring the embarrassingly wet fabric I slid down my legs.

"Put your feet on the edge of the chair." The move exposed me completely, and I flinched as the night breeze brushed against my heated core. Weston pushed out of his chair, tucking himself away as he moved to perch on the end of my lounger.

"God, I almost forgot how pretty your pussy is. Will you give it a stroke?" I could barely breathe, so caught up in his dirty spell that I would have done anything he asked. Not because I was being coerced, but because I wanted it as fiercely as he did. The whole experience was freeing in a way I couldn't describe. My fingers slid easily through my folds, coming away soaking wet as Weston hummed his approval.

"How did that feel, princess? Want to do it again? Or do you need to be filled?"

I moaned, imagining him driving into me hard and fast. I wanted him to own me.

"You'd better fuck yourself with your fingers then, hmm?"

I whimpered, sliding two fingers into my pussy and pumping hard as I circled my clit with my thumb. The wet squelch of my fingers pushing into my body was obscene, and I squirmed against my palm feeling too much and not enough. I added a third finger, curling them inside me as I lifted my hips, chasing the sensation with Weston's filthy words filling my head.

"You're such a good girl, I want you to come all over your fingers. Imagine it's my cock fucking you so deep and hard. I can't wait to taste you again. Come now for me so I can lick you clean."

A scream tore from my throat, and my body trembled against the onslaught of sensation as sparks danced in my vision.

"Such a good girl," he muttered, leaning forward to brush the hair from my face. As my breathing slowed, he took my hand in a gentle grip and sucked my drenched fingers into his mouth. He hummed around the digits as his wicked tongue lapped up every drop of my release.

"Fucking addictive. God, I missed your taste."

He reached down beside him and retrieved my skirt and panties, sliding them over my legs until I was once again covered. The wet fabric was cool and a little uncomfortable, but the kiss he pressed to my lips stole my attention.

"Will you stay the night?"

I wanted to say yes, but as the sweat cooled on my forehead, I realized that we had shared orgasms in a backyard next door to friends we had just had a meal with. There was every chance they'd just heard me come so hard I saw stars and staying the night meant I'd have to see them in the morning.

"Next time," I promised, softening the blow with another kiss before I slid out from underneath him.

The drive home was a blur, my mind vacillating between memories of our shared orgasms outside and self-flagellation at my cowardly retreat. He hadn't been able to completely hide the disappointment on his face as I left his house.

I climbed the stairs to my apartment both physically and emotionally exhausted from the day. I needed eight to ten hours of sleep before I could come up with a plan to apologize for bouncing on Weston after a wonderful night.

My thoughts screeched to a halt as I reached my landing and found an overnight bag and an unwelcome visitor on my doorstep.

"You never answer your phone anymore, so I decided to come for a visit."

"Hi, Mom."

Gia

AFTER A RESTLESS NIGHT'S sleep on my own sofa, because heaven forbid Angela Kennedy should have to sleep anywhere other than the best bed in the house, I woke to my phone vibrating across the table.

"Hey Lydia," I grumbled, scrubbing a hand over my face. My palm came away smeared with foundation and mascara, and I mentally cursed myself for forgetting to do my skin care before bed. I couldn't risk a breakout this close to starting with *Shifting Sands*.

"Clear your calendar, we're touring the set today. You'll meet the cast and crew and officially sign the contract. Congratulations, you did it."

My heart burst into a wild thunder as nerves and excitement battled it out in my stomach. I couldn't believe it was happening today. My first instinct was to call Weston and tell him the news, but could I do that after how I'd left the night before? Would he even care? Parking the depressing thought, I concentrated on Lydia's instructions and repeated them back to make sure I hadn't misheard, then ended the call with a promise to be early. Moving faster than my racing thoughts, I threw myself into the shower, scrubbing and shaving until I sparkled, then slowed down to do my skin care and makeup. I needed to consider my outfit because first impressions mattered. Part of me wanted to wear the dress I'd had on when I met Weston because clearly it was good luck, but in the end I settled for a cream pantsuit. Professional and sophisticated.

"Where are we going?"

I paused in the process of pulling on my shoe as my mother appeared in the doorway, already dressed and ready for the day in a pencil skirt and blouse that was better suited to an office job than a weekend away visiting her daughter.

"I have a set tour to get to. I don't know how long it'll take, but maybe afterward we can go for lunch." Uncomfortably aware of time ticking away, I edged toward the door. Mom mirrored my movements, and I had a sudden vision of making a break for the Uber. I could dive into the passenger seat as they rolled up to the curb, screaming *Go! Go! Go!*

"We'd better get a move on, then. What set is this for? Did you get another medication advertisement? Or was it clothing you did last?" She picked up her purse with an expectant look. Why couldn't she take this kind of interest in Duckie? They could hang out and act superior far away from me. But no. She had chosen to invite herself into one of the most important weeks of my life.

I sighed, casting around for any excuse to keep her from tagging along for the day.

"I did a photo shoot for an athletic brand last week, but this is for a TV show."

Her eyes lit up and I silently cursed myself for showing my hand. "A TV show? Well, aren't you getting all the attention these days? Good thing you're doing it now while you have your looks. You have to work with what you've got. Now, are you driving? I slept terribly with all the paint fumes in that bedroom."

I'd forgotten about my painting project. Oops.

My phone buzzed with an alert that my Uber had arrived while my mother stood in the doorway, set and determined to tag along.

"The Uber is downstairs. If you're coming, I need you to be less... you."

"What a stupid thing to say. Of course I'm me. Everyone loves me."

I retrieved my purse with a sigh of defeat and led the way down to our waiting car.

"You know, my nickname was Angel when I was Gia's age. She's almost as pretty as I was. Shame she didn't get my brains too, though. You know we always get asked if we're sisters? It's very flattering, but you couldn't pay me to be in my late twenties again. Honestly, it's such an awkward age." Mom was in fine form, batting her eyelashes and advising anyone within hearing range of her disappointment in me as a human. The PA who had met us at the gate and acted as escort around the lot glanced at me with a grimace.

I know, buddy. Welcome to my life.

"Marty is filming offsite this morning, but he should be

back before we finish here so you'll have a chance to meet him," he said, cutting in on Mom's self-appreciation speech.

Marty Wiseman had been the director of *Shifting Sands* for the last fifteen years. He'd won so many daytime program awards that it was rumored he'd started donating the statues to the less fortunate. I wasn't sure how true the story was because I was certain I'd read somewhere that the statues were only gold plated, but the fact remained that he was a legend at what he did, and I wasn't just going to meet him, I was going to work with him. Despite the continued prattling beside me, my heart lifted as we moved through the lot and into one of the warehouse-sized buildings.

"Wow," I whispered, looking around at the various interior sets. I could move from the study in Draven's beach house, to his bar hideout, to Thane's bedroom — where he made sweet, respectful love to the heroine of the week. In the far corner, a massive green screen was set up for the scenes requiring special effects.

"Pretty sweet, huh?" The PA, whose name I'd forgotten as soon as he told us because Mom was stressing me out too much to focus, sounded almost as awed as I was. Show business wasn't for everyone, but I knew in my gut that it was for me.

We toured the sound stage, and the hair and makeup rooms before heading toward the trailers and dressing rooms for the cast. Being new, I didn't expect much, so I wasn't surprised when the room he showed me looked like a converted storage closet. I didn't care, though. Because someone had already taped a sign with my name on it to the door. Without a second thought, I pulled out my cell, snapped a photo, and sent it to Weston. A reply came through almost immediately, and I smiled at his response.

> Weston: Congratulations, superstar. You're going to nail it.

"Who are you texting?" Mom asked, reading over my shoulder before I could hide the screen.

"Who's Weston?"

I opened my mouth to tell her it was none of her business, but Mr. helpful PA beat me to it.

"Oh, shit! I thought it was just a rumor. You're really dating Weston Naylor? That's awesome. Do you think he'll come to set? I have the special edition ball Pace released with his signature on it."

"I take it you're an Engines fan?" I asked as Mom side-eyed me.

"Huge. Check it." He hoisted his pant leg high enough to reveal the Chicago Engines steam train mascot.

"Are you harassing our new star with your football obsession, Paulie?" Dressed in neatly pressed slacks and a button down shirt, looking just as good as any of the men he made shine in front of the camera, Marty Wiseman breezed into the room looking like the quintessential silver fox. I didn't need to look at her to know the moment Mom noticed him. A weird, choked noise that sounded almost like a giggle burst from her as she shouldered past me to shake his hand.

"Angela Kennedy. I'm Gia's mother. I know, she gets her looks from me. I was always told I should be an actress, but I wanted to do something useful for the world. I would have been bored repeating lines and standing where I was told because, well, it's not terribly challenging, is it?"

Marty glanced at me, then back at the force of nature

that had birthed me, and gave a practiced smile. "Delighted to meet you. It's always nice to see family supporting cast members with the transition into a new role. Gia." He squeezed Mom's hand and moved around her. Cupping my shoulders gently, he looked me over. "You're more perfect than I could have hoped."

"Thank you." I tried not to twitch under the scrutiny.

Paulie the PA put a hand to his earpiece and turned toward Marty "They're looking for you on sound stage two, sir. And HR is ready for Gia to get contracts signed."

Marty gave us a friendly goodbye and left without fuss as Paulie led us to a suite of offices near the entrance.

"You're dating a football player? Since when?" Mom hissed as we waited to be called in.

"It's new. Can we talk about this later?"

She hummed in disapproval, but let the subject drop until we slid into an Uber to head home.

"I want to meet him," she announced as I buckled my seat belt.

"Who?"

"Weston football player. Whatever his name was. If you're dating someone, I should meet them."

"Why?"

The look she gave me called me an idiot as efficiently as words.

"Because I'm your mother, and I should know the people you're spending time with."

I sighed, not bothering to respond as I rubbed at my eyes. It was so tiring dealing with her. She always managed to simultaneously make me feel five years old and like I was the most stupid person on the planet.

"How's Dad?" I asked instead and settled back in my

seat as she listed all his shortcomings and the reasons he was lucky to have her.

It was mid-afternoon by the time we arrived back at my apartment, and I was thoroughly done with the day. Mom had insisted on stopping off in the shopping district for lunch at one of the finer restaurants where she criticized every food choice I made.

"I need to pack my bag. My flight leaves at six PM," she announced, breezing through my front door and heading toward my bedroom. "I don't suppose you'll bother driving me to the airport, so can you order a car for me?"

Gladly.

In a thankfully short amount of time, she was packed up and ready to head out.

"By the way, we're hosting Thanksgiving this year. Bring your boyfriend so he can meet the family."

I'd been so close to avoiding the discussion. So close. And then it hit me.

"Weston has a game over Thanksgiving. We won't be able to make it down."

"It's fine," she said, hoisting her bag through the front door.

"We'll move the date so we can celebrate together."

The door slammed behind her, and I felt the weight of her presence lift off my shoulders as her footsteps faded in the corridor.

I'd survived her whirlwind visit this time, but now I faced a new problem.

Convincing my fake boyfriend to meet the family.

CHAPTER
TWELVE

Weston

Georgie: How's Florida?

Weston: Hot and wet.

Georgie: Like me?

Weston: Fuck, princess. You're in a mood, aren't you?

Georgie: Sorry. I feel like I need to butter you up before I ask a huge favor that I've been putting off asking, and you should absolutely say no to, but I really hope you'll say yes.

Weston: Color me intrigued.

> Georgie: Is there any chance you feel like celebrating a late Thanksgiving in Texas while you protect me from my nightmare family? Before you ask, I'm absolutely throwing you to the wolves and asking you to wrap yourself in bacon first.

> Weston: I don't know if that was meant to sound kinky, or if I've just been missing you, but seeing as saving you is one of my favorite hobbies, there's no way I'd miss a chance to meet the family that puts the fun in dysfunctional.

> Georgie: They're really not fun. But thank you.

> Georgie: I miss you too, BTW.

I GRINNED as I tucked my phone into my gym bag and headed for the bus to the hotel. Between Georgia starting on set, and back-to-back away games for the team, we'd barely had a chance to see each other. Our fake relationship was still in place, but the less I got to see her, the more I realized I wished it were real and that we could make the time to spend together. Our text conversations had been the highlight of my day for weeks, but I hadn't worked up the balls to tell her how I felt.

Life was unpredictable, and I didn't think I'd survive getting close to Georgia and having her walk away from me like Harmony did.

"You look deep in thought," Christian said, dropping into the seat beside me as the bus trundled out of the parking lot.

"Life, love, and next steps, my brother," I said, watching the stadium recede into the distance.

Christian hummed, flipping his cell in his hands. "I get that. How is everything? Gia, your shoulder... you?"

I wanted to brush him off. Make like everything was sweet and move on, but it seemed like I mightn't have been the only one going through something, so I went with something close to honesty.

"Things are good on the surface, but I guess I'm wondering if I can trust it, you know? I thought things were good with Harmony, but then..." I shrugged. Christian had been there through every step of the last year, and had seen me rebuild not just from the injury but from the heartbreak.

"Marina likes Gia." It was said with the resolve that Amber would use to convince me cookies were better than cake. It was an absolute, and therefore impossible to refute.

"Does she?"

Christian glanced at me, then back at his hands as he continued to flip the phone over and over. His heel tapped out a staccato rhythm in time to his bouncing knee.

"She's mentioned it a few times when I pick Zara up from her house. Just little things, but she likes how you are with Gia. She says you smile more, and that you both deserve some happiness."

"That's really nice of her to say—"

"She never liked Harmony."

Christian met my eye with a firm look, like he wasn't sure whether he'd dropped the social equivalent of a nuclear bomb.

"I don't know if she has some therapist superpower, or she's just really good at reading people, but she never liked her. It wasn't like she was rude about it, and never to her, but you know how Marina gets quiet around people she doesn't trust. I dunno, man. I guess what I'm trying to say is that I know you have every reason to expect this relationship to bomb the same way your last one did, but the people around you are rooting for you. You both deserve to be happy."

I wondered how they would feel if they knew the whole thing was a lie. That we'd let them believe in something that was nothing more than a business transaction. A mutually beneficial arrangement that, admittedly, kept blurring the professional lines.

It should have ended when Georgia got the job, but the thought of giving up what little I had of her felt like too much of a sacrifice. It was too soon. I needed more time. More of her.

So I insisted we keep going. And now I was going to meet her family and lie to a new group of people.

Was it really a lie, though?

It may have started that way, but I knew Georgia now, and she knew me. Christian was right; she was nothing like Harmony. Despite being in the public eye, she didn't seek out the media. I had the sneaking suspicion that she often forgot everyone else in the room when we were together. And wasn't that one hell of an ego boost.

Christian clapped me on the shoulder and pushed out of his seat. "Whatever happens, just know we've always got your back, bro."

I caught his wrist as he moved toward the back of the bus.

"Same here, man. If there's anything going on that you need to talk out, I'm here."

He gave me a nod and moved back a few rows to sit with a rookie player who'd had a rough couple of games.

We pulled into our hotel and I made my way up to my room with visions of a shower and room service dancing in my head. I'd had a shower in the stadium, but I'd Googled the hotel we were in and I had two words. Rainfall. Showerhead. Hell yes.

Half an hour later I was warm and relaxed from my shower and accepting a pepperoni pizza I'd called up from the kitchen. I stretched out on my bed and bit into the first greasy slice when my phone pinged.

> Georgie: What does a fake girlfriend have to do around here to get an unsolicited dick pic?

I choked on my mouthful, spraying cheese across the bedspread and trying to regain my breath. Life was never dull talking to my Georgie girl, and I wondered what chain of thoughts had led her to the text.

> Weston: She just needs to ask. Also, how did we get onto the subject of unsolicited dick pics?

> Georgie: Well... after your text before about being hot and wet I went down a rabbit hole looking up weather trends in Florida, which led me to a site that showcases daily 'Florida Man' content (I hope you aren't going out drinking there, BTW, these guys are insane)

> Georgie: Anyway, one of the stories was a Florida woman who received an unsolicited dick pic from a guy, so she hunted him down and removed the dick to teach him about consent. Anyway, then I thought that you'd never do anything like that without consent, but if I asked for it you might. So I texted you.

I laughed, setting my dinner aside in favor of this much more interesting conversation.

> Weston: It sounds like you've been busy.

> Georgie: I've been something. So can I get one?

> Weston: And what do you plan to do with it?

The dancing dots appeared and disappeared for a drawn-out moment.

> Georgie: Show me yours and I'll show you mine.

> Weston: You're being delightfully bratty tonight, princess.

> Georgie: I'm not-so-delightfully horny, Weston. Don't make me Google Weston Naylor ass dot com. There are whole forums dedicated to how good you look in your uniform, FYI.

> Weston: Good to know.

I glanced at the locked door, then at the semi I was already sporting. I liked that Georgia was open about appreciating my body. I worked hard for it. Plus, it felt more like she liked me for me. Not the sports star whose name could open doors. Just Weston.

Without further hesitation, I ditched the plush robe I slipped on after my shower and grabbed my phone. My dick got harder as I tried to take the best picture I could, thinking about what she would do once I sent it. Would she fuck herself with her fingers like she did on my patio?

Rub her clit raw while thinking of riding me?

"Fuck."

I gripped my erection and gave it a hard stroke as I hit send.

Immediately, my phone rang. I answered without bothering to look at the caller ID.

"Is that what you wanted, princess?"

Through the line, I heard her breath hitch.

"What are you doing, Georgie girl?"

"Touching myself."

I groaned, squeezing the base of my dick hard as it kicked in my hand.

"Set the scene for me."

There was a rustle of fabric and a sigh. "I'm naked in my room. It's a bit distracting in here because I started to paint it a few weeks ago and never finished, but my bed is comfortable—"

"Princess," I cut in.

"Yes?"

"Turn off the light."

"Okay."

There were sounds of movement through the line and then a whump as she landed back in bed.

"Done."

"Good. Now, tell me how you feel. Where are your hands? Where do you want my hands?"

Her moan sent goosebumps racing over my skin as I brought the memory of her naked form to mind.

"You're pinching my nipple," she murmured. "Your other hand is around my throat."

"Do you like my hand there?"

She hummed. "I wish you'd do it to me more often. It makes me feel safe. Owned."

The word lit me up from the inside out. Fucking hell, I wanted to own her.

"Put your hand between your legs and tell me how wet you are."

Her breath stuttered, a small "ah" falling out as I waited for her response. Instead of telling me, she must have moved the speaker, because deliciously filthy noises came down the line as she slid her fingers into her wet pussy.

"Fuck yourself like I would if I was there," I murmured, matching my strokes to the little mewls falling from her lips.

"Imagine they're my fingers inside you. Can you feel me?"

"Yes." Her breath was coming in faster pants, her sheets crinkling as she chased the high I wanted her to feel.

"Rub your clit with your other hand, baby. I want to hear you come apart for me."

My balls tightened, a warning tingle in my lower back telling me I was seconds from blowing. I needed to get her there quickly.

"Be a good girl and come for me. Now."

Her voice broke on a cry, and I let my own orgasm barrel through me, making no attempt to stifle the grunts and groans of pleasure. Letting her hear it all.

The room was quiet in the aftermath, except for the sound of her breath through the phone as I reached for napkins on my nightstand to clean myself up.

"You okay over there, Georgie girl?"

"Mm-hmm."

"Still need to search my ass on the internet?"

Her chuckle was deep and satisfied. I wanted to record it so I could play it back again and again while I slept alone in this hotel room.

"Maybe later."

"Brat." I grinned as she chuckled again. Overhead, the

cooling system kicked in, sending a cold gust across my overheated skin. "I might need another shower," I muttered, dropping the soiled napkins in a wastebasket in the corner of the room.

"Sounds lovely. I think I'm going to just fall asleep right here."

"Did I wear you out, princess?"

The rustle of sheets was all the response I got, and as I pictured her sleeping naked my worn-out dick made a valiant attempt to rally.

"Sweet dreams, princess. Thanks for calling me."

I ended the call and wandered into the bathroom for round two with the shower, feeling both elated and grounded in a way I hadn't for a long time.

Weston

THE CHRISTMAS DECORATIONS were already up as we moved through the crowds at O'Hare Airport, headed for the domestic terminal. The plan had been to arrive early for our flight to Austin, but when I arrived at Georgia's house, I'd found her elbow deep in tiny, sticky diamonds. Apparently, she'd heard on a podcast that diamond art was good for mindfulness and had decided to give it a shot. I had no idea how she'd ended up with the jewels stuck to her face, but it was an adorable look that she didn't appreciate me pointing out as she threw herself into the shower to get ready. Somehow, we'd managed to arrive in time for check in, but we wouldn't be spending time in the flight lounge. Which seemed a shame because my girl could have used a drink. She was practically vibrating with nerves at the thought of seeing her family.

"Don't forget to breathe, princess."

She strode ahead, her heels clicking out an anxious rhythm as I caught her hand.

"Hey. It'll be alright, okay? I'm right here with you."

She blinked wild eyes at me, the words settling in slowly until she dropped her shoulders with a nod. "I wish I didn't have to expose you to them, but if we don't go there, they're sure to come to us and that would be infinitely worse."

I threaded my fingers through hers and gave a gentle squeeze. We set off at a more measured pace, making it through security and to our gate with time to spare.

"When do you have to be back on set?" I asked, hoping to distract her.

"Ahh... next week, I think. But I have a fight scene to learn before then, so I need to be home before the weekend."

We were booked to fly back the following evening. I'd suggested we spend some time exploring while we were there, but Georgia was adamant that an escape plan was best. Her exact words.

At this point I wasn't sure how I'd react to meeting her family. They'd obviously caused her a lot of distress over the years and the part of me who liked to come to her rescue had visions of knocking out her parents on sight dancing through my head.

A voice over the speaker announced our flight was boarding first class and business. Tugging on Georgia's hand, I pulled her into the queue.

"Why are we lining up? They aren't boarding us... wait. What did you do?"

I gave her my best estimation of an innocent look, but honestly, she was the actor here, not me. "Economy doesn't give me enough leg room."

She rolled her eyes, shaking her head as she tried and failed to suppress a smile.

Yes, I had let her think we were paying for our own tickets, but she had to realize I wouldn't let her reimburse me, even if I had been inclined to spend two hours cramped into tiny seats with someone reclining the chair in front of me so they lay across my knees. Not to mention the chances of me being recognized were higher. No thank you.

"You cheated."

"I did."

"Thank you."

We strolled down the air bridge and made our way to the comfortable seating of business class. Georgia took the window seat and became engrossed in the comings and goings of the ground crew as I retrieved a couple of pillows and a blanket from the overhead locker.

The distraction of business class wore off as our plane taxied across the tarmac, and by the time we hit cruising altitude, Georgia was back to fretting about Thanksgiving.

I flagged down a stewardess and requested two glasses of wine, passing one to Georgia and urging her to take a sip and lie back.

"There's nothing we can do about what will or won't happen when we get there, but for right now, let's enjoy ourselves."

She obeyed as beautifully as ever, but it was apparent her mind hadn't settled. Once her glass was empty, I unfolded the blanket and spread it across both our laps, then offered her a pillow for her head.

"I'm not going to be able to sleep on a two-hour flight, Weston. Thank you for trying."

"Not what I had in mind, princess."

Her eyes shot to mine as she registered the growl in my tone.

That's right. I know how to make you relax.

I slid one hand beneath the blanket, squeezing her knee. Without further instruction, she made room for me, and I sent up a prayer of gratitude for her preference for skirts and dresses.

Moving slowly to avoid drawing attention, I rubbed a knuckle over the panel of her panties, giving her a warning look as a small gasp escaped her lips.

"You're going to have to stay quiet for me, Georgie girl. Can you do that?"

She nodded, eyes wide as she tilted her hips into my knuckle.

"Good girl," I muttered and slipped my hand beneath the fabric. Warm, slick flesh slid beneath my fingertips, and I gritted my teeth against a possessive growl.

She was always ready for me.

"I'm starting to think you have an exhibitionist kink."

Her plump lips parted on a silent breath as I pushed two fingers deep into her pussy.

Checking the cabin for unwanted eyes, I ground the heel of my palm against her clit while pumping into her in long strokes. The row across from us was mercifully empty, and a glance behind us confirmed the occupants had already donned headphones and buried their heads in their tablets.

"Does the thought of getting caught make you wet?"

She wrapped one small hand around my wrist, using the leverage to grind against my hand, her brow furrowed as she concentrated on her pleasure.

She was beautiful like this. Undone. Focused on taking what she wanted. What she deserved.

A small gasp was all the noise she made as her back arched in a beautiful curve, her muscles squeezing my fingers like a vise. I stroked her through the trembles that rocked her body and waited until she released a final contented breath before pulling away.

Her skin was flushed a beautiful pink, the color giving a glow to her cheeks that I wanted to photograph. She rolled her head on the headrest and settled heavy, satiated eyes on me.

"Thank you. You're so good to me," she said, her voice dreamy, like maybe she could take the nap she'd denied earlier.

"I like taking care of you," I said, kissing her on the nose.

She hummed a happy noise and closed her eyes. The sigh she released as she settled in told me that for now her stresses had been held at bay.

As the plane started its descent and the seat belt sign pinged on above us, Georgia stirred from her nap, rubbing a sleepy hand over her face like she could cast out the roar of the engines and the stewards making preparations for landing.

"Time to wake up, princess. We're just about there," I murmured. "Orgasms really wipe you out, huh? At least I'll know what to do if you ever struggle with sleep."

"Happy for you to give me a sleep aid any time," she said, and cracked an eyelid.

"You just have to ask."

Once we'd disembarked, we fought our way through the crowded airport to the baggage claim, grabbed a taxi out front, and were on our way to our belated Thanksgiving celebration.

"There's still time to bail, you know," Georgia said in a small voice, wringing her hands.

"Not going to happen. I'm in this with you. I'm shooting for the best fake boyfriend ever award."

My joke fell flat, if the way her shoulders curled in was any indication. I felt powerless to help as she pulled into herself in a way I hadn't seen since the first day we met.

Georgia was a big personality. Selfless, despite the circumstances we found ourselves in, and impulsive in a way that kept life exciting. But when she felt uncomfortable, the voice in her head that told her she wasn't good enough was loud.

We pulled up to a beautiful two-story craftsman in the suburbs sometime later, and while I appreciated the architecture, Georgia pulled further into herself.

"Are you sure *you* don't want to bail?" I asked, giving her hand a squeeze.

She shook her head and thanked the driver as she slipped out onto the curb.

"Let's get this over with," she muttered, straightening her dress. With every step she took toward the door, the Georgia I knew seemed to recede. Her shoulders were squared, her stride long, and by the time we reached the door, she looked ready for battle. Without bothering to knock, she strode inside, pausing at the sight of a huge golden retriever who lifted its head from where it lay in the front hall.

"Bessie."

At the sound of its name, the dog lumbered to its feet and trotted over to Georgia who immediately dropped to the floor. Golden strands of fluff floated through the air as the beast crawled all over Georgia's prone form, licking and nuzzling my giggling fake girlfriend.

I leaned against the wall wearing a small grin as I watched her greet the one family member she clearly missed. The moment was broken up by the arrival of a petite woman in a black dress and apron who took one look at the beautiful scene in front of us and clicked her tongue in annoyance. "Get off the ground, Gia. You're an absolute mess. I wish you'd think things through just once. Now you're going to be covered in dog hair for dinner."

As Georgia scrambled to her feet looking chagrined, my presence must have registered for the woman because her demeanor flipped immediately to gracious host.

"You must be the football player. Aren't you handsome? I'm Gia's mother. I know, hard to believe. People always think Gia and I are sisters. You can call me Angela. Come, come. Let me introduce you to my husband. Can I get you a drink?"

I glanced back at Georgia as her mother ushered me through the kitchen and out to the back patio. Her face was a blank mask. It hurt my heart to see that despite the fact her body was with us, her mind had taken off for somewhere else.

Where they couldn't hurt her.

CHAPTER
FOURTEEN

Gia

I PICKED at a piece of dog fur on my dress as I sat beside Weston on the back deck. One of the few silver linings of the visit was being able to sit outside for a meal. We'd left a 25-degree day behind in Chicago in favor of a much more pleasant 60-degree day here.

Look at me discussing the weather with myself to avoid thinking about the proximity of my family.

I rolled my eyes at myself and tried to tune in to Dad showing off his football knowledge for Weston.

"I can't say I particularly follow Chicago, but I was watching when you injured yourself last season. Good to see you back on the field this year, son. It's important to pick yourself up and keep going."

"Thank you, sir. Honestly, I'm just happy to be back playing with my team. You never know what life is going to throw at you." He reached under the table and squeezed my thigh. "Sometimes the best things have nothing to do with sports."

A clatter and the sound of claws on floorboards announced another arrival, and I braced myself for the coming unpleasantness.

"Sounds like Blair's here," Dad announced, like the party could finally begin.

In a riot of curls, towing a dark-haired man who was several inches shorter than Weston, my sister burst onto the back deck and destroyed any semblance of peace we'd had.

"Holy shit! Cian O'Leary!" Dad pushed out of his chair in a rush, his hand leading the way for a firm shake.

"What are you doing here? Duckie, you didn't tell me you were bringing Cian O'Leary to the house. How's the head, son? That was one hell of a knock you took last night."

Weston and I were forgotten in the excitement of Blair's arrival and some accident Cian had apparently been in recently.

As Dad fan-girled about Duckie's date, Weston introduced himself to my sister. When she reached across the table, it took everything in me to keep from knocking her hand away. I didn't want them to touch. I didn't want her to take him from me. He was mine. And not just because he was a well-known football player, but because he was Weston.

Except he wasn't mine, was he?

What would they say if they knew our relationship was fake? I needed to do whatever it took to avoid finding out.

"How much did you have to pay him to come here?" I nodded toward Cian, in case she wasn't sure who I meant.

Weston shot me a curious look, but the more I thought about it, the better the idea became.

Deflect, redirect, stay safe.

If everyone was questioning the validity of Duckie's relationship, they wouldn't look too closely at mine.

"I didn't."

I snorted. Of course not. What was the saying? The girl you brought home to meet the parents? That was Blair. She was smart and successful. Plain looking, but that just meant this guy liked her for who she is. It also meant that she wouldn't be worrying about Botox and fillers in a few years like I would have to. Like Mom already did.

"Oh! Hey, you play for the Engines, right?" she asked, drawing Weston's attention again.

"Yeah, I do. I play tight end. Do you watch?"

"Whenever I can, the hockey season keeps me busy though."

"That's sport, isn't it?" They shared a knowing smile and a part of me curled up and died. He liked her. Probably more than me. Everyone liked her more.

"Hey, Cian. Do you know why Blair is called Duckie? Tell him, Blair. It's funny. It's because she's the ugly duckling. Get it?"

My stomach burned at the look Weston gave me, but whatever. I wasn't saying anything people didn't already know. I suddenly wanted nothing more than to crawl into a corner somewhere and cry. Weston and I had been fake dating for months, and even though I knew I wasn't good enough for him, there was a small part that was desperate for him to want me. Not just for sex when we blurred the lines of our deal, but always. That just wasn't in the cards for me.

Instead, I chose carbs. A large scoop of potatoes from

the bowl in the center of the table hit my plate with a loud plop. Mom clicked her tongue.

"Do you really need that, Georgia? You won't keep your job long if you stack on more weight."

Why did she have to be right? My face warmed as I returned the majority of the serving to the bowl and picked at the salad leaves instead.

I hated it here.

The table fell into an uncomfortable silence as everyone ate until Mom heaved a dramatic sigh and dropped her cutlery.

"It really was nice of you to be here with Blair today, but I can't in good conscience let you get her hopes up. If this is transactional, that's fine, but if not... this is just cruel."

"What... do you mean?" Cian asked.

"Well, all I'm saying is that if you expect us to believe that an athlete like you would be interested in someone like her, then clearly something else is going on. I don't like deception and I'd hate to think you were using her."

Holy shit.

I cast a quick look at Weston, terrified we'd be next on the list to be called out by my bitch of a mother, but her focus was solely on the hockey player.

Thank god.

"That's enough. None of you appreciate this woman, and I'm not going to let her sit here and listen to you belittle her anymore." Cian's words were sweet, and everything I wished someone would say to my parents on my behalf, but as he laid down the law and dragged Duckie out of the house, it occurred to me that no one ever would.

Mom pushed out of her chair, ready to chase them down, but Dad came to the rescue. Like always. The silence descended once more, heavy with the weight of things that couldn't be changed. I caught Weston's eye, ready to make our excuses, and found a profound sadness looking back at me.

"Thank you for dinner. We should really be going," I said without breaking eye contact.

"Don't be stupid. We haven't had dessert yet," Mom spat, smoothing her apron.

Dad said nothing, taking an intense interest in his hands as I stood and pushed my chair in neatly.

"I don't think it's a good idea for me to have dessert. I'd hate to sacrifice my figure for a piece of pie."

Tears burned at the back of my eyes. Screw them all. I didn't bother to see if Weston followed me out of the house, just stalked right on through, without even acknowledging the whine of query Bessie gave me as I stomped past.

It was time for me to grow up.

I'd relied on Weston too much recently and had gotten used to having someone in my corner, but he'd get bored with me sooner rather than later. Witnessing Cian and Blair together as a united front had broken something inside of me.

"Georgie," Weston called, jogging down the front walk toward me. "Wait up. Are you okay?"

"I couldn't stay there any longer. They're just awful."

A car rolled by slowly, the crunch of tires against gravel loud in the twilight. In the distance, crickets chirped as a cool breeze swept through the space between us.

"I think Cian had the right idea with the no contact thing," he said, closing the distance to wrap his arms around me. I stepped out of reach before he could make contact.

"No, you don't get it. That means I have to deal with them on my own. No distractions." I paced away from him, trying to wrangle the runaway train of my catastrophic thoughts.

"I'm trapped. Duckie gets to live her perfect life with her perfect boyfriend while I get stuck here."

"I wish you wouldn't call her Duckie. It's not like you to be so unkind."

"It's exactly like me. Don't pretend you know me, Weston. Just because we pretended to date for a while and shared a few orgasms doesn't mean you know anything about me."

Why couldn't I shut up? The words poured out of me like poison. My insecurity not just pushing him away, but using an old cannon to launch him into space to ensure maximum fallout.

"Georgia—"

"Don't Georgia me. We said we'd come to a mutual decision when it was best to stop this fake relationship, and I think that time is now. Have a nice life, Weston. I hope I made a good story for you to tell someday when you want a real girlfriend again."

I squared my shoulders and turned away, making it halfway to the neighbor's driveway before I realized I'd made a significant tactical error.

Stalking back toward him, I pulled my phone out of my pocket and searched our return flight for the following day.

"We still need to fly home. I'm sure I can move my seat away from you when we change our flights."

The airport had room on a flight two hours later, and I chose a seat in economy to ensure maximum separation from Weston and his beautiful life.

I needed to get used to my place again, anyway.

CHAPTER
FIFTEEN

Weston

WE WERE GETTING our asses kicked.

The Dakota Dragons had come to play today. Their silver and navy jerseys looked extra shiny, their defensive line impenetrable. But even if they had shown up to our turf in flip flops and half injured, they'd still be ahead. Our team wasn't gelling today. Every play felt clunky, and the one field goal we'd attempted had come off Jeffries's boot wrong and gone wide.

I felt like my mood had infected the team, and the Dragons had never been a team to let their opposition's weakness slide.

I jogged off the field, passing our defensive line on their way out, and knocked fists with Dawson, our linebacker.

He slapped my back as he continued onto the field, clapping his hands to rally the team.

Don't do it.

I glanced toward the field level suite where Cami and

Marina sat watching us bomb the game. I could almost feel their disappointment in us from here. The seat beside Cami was glaringly empty, like it had been the week before, after our return from the disastrous Thanksgiving dinner in Texas. Despite having replayed the conversation in her parents' driveway over in my head to the point of insanity, I still couldn't see how it had all gone wrong.

It was obvious to me that Georgia's parents were toxic as fuck. They'd clearly played their daughters against each other for years. Blair honestly seemed cool, and I'd looked Cian up after I got home and couldn't get out of my own head. He was a well-respected player with a reputation of having a cool head on the ice. I could respect that.

It hurt my heart to think that Georgia was so used to being under attack in her own home that everyone had become the enemy.

Apparently, that now included me.

"You're thinking really hard over there." Christian moved up the bench toward me and held out a bottle of water. I took a drink and tried to focus on the game, but the weight of his attention dragged me back.

"Can't help but notice this is the second game Gia has missed. That combined with the black cloud you've been sporting tells me something's up."

"Shouldn't you be watching the game?" I asked, tipping my chin toward the field as Dakota made their second down.

"It's done. We'll do better next time, but it would help if we knew what was going on with our tight end."

I winced at the confirmation my miserable attitude was affecting the team.

"Come on, man. Talk to me."

"She called it off."

Christian blew out a hard breath and sat back. "Ah, man. That sucks. I'm sorry. What happened? You guys seemed really happy together."

"We weren't."

"Happy?"

"Together."

"What do you mean?"

Christian had turned his body completely toward me, any attempt at looking like he was monitoring the game gone in light of my reveal. An icy breeze blew through the stadium, and I shivered at the warning of impending snow.

"It was fake. The relationship. A lie that got out of hand, and we just kind of rolled with it until it didn't work anymore."

"Bullshit."

Out on the field, the Dragons got their first down. The clock ticked relentlessly toward the end of the game, and I wondered how quickly I could get out of here. My shoulder twinged in agreement, reminding me I needed to buy a new heat pack on my way home.

"There was nothing fake about the way you two were together."

Christian was like a dog with a bone when I just wanted to bury the thing. Georgia had left. Same as Harmony. What did he not get about that?

"She was using my name as leverage to get the role on *Shifting Sands*. Mission accomplished. There's nothing else to say about it."

Christian cursed.

"I'm sorry, bro. You're too good. I really thought she liked you, and I know you liked her."

I shifted on the bench, worried that it hadn't come out right. It wasn't fair to put it all on Georgia.

"It wasn't like that. We both agreed to it. I think we both just got caught up in the lie for a while. I'm sorry we weren't honest with you guys, I've been feeling shitty about that, too."

We watched the clock tick away as Dakota set up for their fourth play.

"Did you tell her you wanted it to be real?"

Why wouldn't he let it drop?

"I told her the opposite. I didn't want a relationship. After Harmony, I just couldn't risk losing someone else. That breakup hurt almost more than the injury."

"And how'd that work out for you?"

It hadn't. I'd fallen for Georgia just as surely as if we had been real. The ache in my chest told me I'd fucked up, but I didn't know how to fix it. The past two weeks had been an unbearable mix of loneliness and depression. I'd avoided leaving the house as much as possible because I knew Marina would be lying in wait to make me talk. Instead, she'd sent Christian.

"You've been spending too much time with my neighbor," I muttered.

Christian's snort was drowned out by the final whistle, and I breathed a sigh of relief that we were almost done for the day. The visiting team went wild for their win, while disappointed Engines fans were more subdued as they filed out of the stadium. Fuck. I hated letting the fans down.

We made our way down to the locker rooms, and I took my time in the shower, setting the water as hot as I could stand to burn away the conversation I'd had with Christian.

The problem was, I knew he was right.

I'd been hiding from my feelings for Georgia for a while, and when she left, it was easier to let her go than take a chance that maybe the reason she left was because she was as scared of wanting more as I was.

I had a support network, but what did she have?

I knew from covert questioning that none of the girls had heard from her in the last two weeks, and it wasn't like she'd be asking her mom for guidance, so who could she go to?

An idea formed in my mind as I pulled on my street clothes and headed for the door.

"Naylor. You got a minute?" Coach Laudner called from the door to the friends and family room.

"Sure, Coach." I ignored the way my heart hitched in hope that maybe Georgia was behind the door and pasted on a smile.

"I'd like you to meet Wayne Desmond," Coach said, indicating a dark-skinned man with shaved head and height and bulk to match my own. Of course, I knew of the man, he'd been one of the greats when I was playing in college, and had established a successful career commentating in recent years.

"It's good to meet you, sir," I said, shaking his hand and throwing Coach a curious look. I appreciated the introduction, but wasn't sure why it was happening.

"You too, son. How's the shoulder?"

"Good as new," I lied and followed him over to one of the sofas.

"Good to hear. You must be wondering why I've asked to meet with you. I'll be honest, I've been looking into mentorship opportunities, and I recently met someone who put your name forward."

I glanced at Coach, whose creased brow told me he was as confused as I was.

"I have a daughter," Wayne said, sitting back and kicking an ankle onto his opposite knee.

"She's mad for all those daytime TV shows. Anyway, we were touring a set earlier this week and were able to meet some of the cast."

My stomach started to crawl as I reached a conclusion that sounded insane. Had Georgia advocated for me? Why? How would that conversation have even come about?

"That girlfriend of yours is something else. I don't even know how we started talking about the mentorship, but before the end of the tour, I'd already agreed to meet with you. I'll admit, son. I knew your stats, but it wasn't until she made the suggestion that I really looked into you. She was right. You have the experience and the connections in the league to be a great commentator. I don't want to jinx your season, but if it's something you'd consider when you're looking at the big R, have your people call mine and we can set up another meeting. What do you say?"

I stared at Wayne Desmond like he was speaking a foreign language. A career shift to commentating had never crossed my mind. There were only so many positions available, and those who had them rarely left except in instances of retirement or death. It was a dream position, and the fact that Georgia seemed to be the catalyst made it difficult to compute.

"When did you meet her?"

Maybe this had happened a while ago, and he'd only just been in a position to make the offer. These things would take time to research and confirm I was a good candidate, right?

"Last week. I know it seems sudden, and please know I'm not expecting you to leave the league tomorrow and take up the mic, but I wanted to test the waters off the record before we started writing up contracts."

Last week.

After Thanksgiving, then.

I needed to see Georgia. Ask her if she was as miserable without me as I was without her, but I stopped. I'd left her alone for two weeks without a word because she'd pushed me away and hurt my feelings. I needed a plan. But first, I needed to get out of here.

"Thank you, sir. I have no intention of retiring before the end of this season, but I'm interested in discussing this further down the line."

The rest of the discussion was a blur as we exchanged numbers and Wayne wished us well for the rest of the season. I excused myself as soon as I was able and packed up my things, ready to head out and call an emergency meeting of my nearest and dearest.

We had under two weeks until Christmas, and I needed to lift my game and prove to my fake girlfriend that our connection was real.

Gia

HEAVY HITTER *in entertainment questioned in relation to rape allegations.*

Denny Hayes's turtle-like face leered out of the phone screen at me from where it lay on the kitchen table. Someone had spoken out about him. Someone was doing something about it, and as I sat beside my cooling coffee going over the article again, all I could think was: why hadn't I done something too?

Why couldn't I now?

The thought settled in, bringing with it a combination of terror and joy, like I'd never experienced before. Four actresses had already come forward to tell their stories of coercion and assault, and the article speculated there may be more allegations in the coming days. These women were getting justice for something that was taken from them in a vulnerable time, and I could speak up with them.

With growing excitement, I called Lydia to bring her up to speed.

"That's the most stupid thing I've ever heard. You'll tank your career. Do you like working, Gia? Because if you do this, no one will hire you again. You'll be serving burgers in a Wendy's by this time next week."

"But don't you think it's important—"

"It's important you shut your mouth and do as you're told. Don't make this about you. I've worked too hard to get you where you are for you to tank the opportunity by crying wolf with the rest of those attention whores."

Ice slid down my spine as I caught my balance on the table in front of me.

Lydia knew damn well what had happened with Denny. She had been the one to pick me up and put me in the shower after the incident. The one who encouraged me to accept the job I'd 'earned' and keep quiet about the audition process.

She'd enabled my abuser, and he'd gone on to hurt others.

"You're fired."

The words slid out without much thought, but like the decision to speak out, I had no intention of changing course once they were said.

"You can't do that."

"There's a clause in your contract that states you will act in the interests of your client in all things. You didn't act in my interest after I was assaulted. You didn't act in my interest when you repeatedly called me stupid and undermined my wishes. You've only done what would further your own career, and that ends here. I deserve to have someone in my corner that isn't waiting to put a knife in my back."

Without letting her speak, I ended the call and collapsed into a chair.

I'd have to speak to a lawyer and make sure I could legally break the contract we had. Also, a call to HR would be important. I'd have to represent my own interests until I found someone new to work with. There was a lot to do, but I felt lighter than I had since...

Well, since I'd blown up my fake relationship with Weston.

The thought brought a wave of sadness with it, and I swallowed through a sudden thickening in my throat. I'd looked back over our text conversations so many times in the last couple of weeks that I could have recited them verbatim.

I'd watched his last two games in my room, under the covers, like it was a secret no one could know. He hadn't been playing as well as usual, and the fact that the blame for that lay at my feet too was just another blow.

I was managing to ruin his life even when I wasn't with him.

A knock at my door shook me out of my miserable thoughts.

I wondered if Lydia had decided to come and berate me in person, but when I looked through the peephole, it was a different brunette glaring back at me.

"I know you're in there. Let us in."

I considered ignoring Cami, but the very real fear of her kicking in my door had me opening things up before she got any bright ideas.

"Why are you in your PJs at midday? Go get dressed. You're coming with us to the ball park." Cami glanced around the living space, taking in the half-finished projects that littered my coffee table and sofa, and the general state of disarray my entire life was in.

"Nice place."

I snorted. "Why are you here?"

I'd ended things with Weston weeks ago and left the group chat. It wasn't right to try to keep his friends after we gave up the charade, so I'd cut ties.

"You've been MIA for ages, and Weston's miserable. My superior deductive reasoning tells me that one, or both of you have fucked up, and you need some girl time to get your head on straight. Ridley and Marina are meeting us at the diamond, so chop chop. Put on clothes you can run in because I'm going to teach you to play God's game."

I wasn't really in the mood to be social. Or play sports of any kind. But I also wasn't going to deny Cami when she was in this mood.

"Have you ever thought about running a boot camp?" I grumbled as I slinked into my bedroom and pulled out some of the activewear I'd been allowed to keep from the *Elite Mind* shoot.

"I have," she said, leaning against the doorframe and watching as I slid into a pair of black sweat pants. "But I'm thinking about teaching men to pitch properly instead. It'll be so much more satisfying watching them break."

I chuckled at her wicked grin and rifled through my closet for some running shoes.

"You don't have to talk about what happened if you don't want to, but we're all here for you if you need to get it out."

Cami's face was softer than I'd ever seen it, and the compassion threatened to break down the walls I'd built. Before I could respond, she straightened and took a step backward.

"Full disclosure, I can only speak for me and Ridley. Marina will absolutely get you to talk."

"Duly noted." I finished getting ready and headed out the door with Cami a few minutes later, sliding into the passenger seat of her car with a sigh.

"I thought you guys wouldn't want me around if Weston and I weren't a thing," I admitted as she pulled into traffic.

"Babe, that's the first dumb thing I've ever heard you say."

THE WELCOME WAS warm when we walked onto the baseball diamond in a park close to where Weston and Marina lived. Even Zara and Amber took a break from perusing the picnic basket someone had brought to come and say hello.

"Have you ever played baseball before?" Zara asked eagerly, her eyes shining with excitement. "Aunt Cami is kickass. She's a better pitcher than any of the players in the men's league."

"It's true, but don't say kickass. Your father will kill us if you use language like that around him," Marina admonished with a gentle smile.

I looked around the diamond, which was muddy from the rain overnight, and back at the women who were laughing and warming up like it wasn't a miracle we weren't standing knee deep in snow.

"You couldn't have staged this intervention in a nice warm cafe, or at least somewhere we won't end up covered in mud?" I asked, only half joking.

"It's ok. Mum says life is messy, but it's better to have to take a bath than miss out on the experience for a silly thing like staying clean," Amber said, giving me a toothy grin before running off after Zara like she hadn't just dropped a philosophical bomb on my head.

Had I been keeping myself on the sidelines to avoid getting messy?

"I need to talk to Weston," I muttered.

"Later. For now, let's play ball." Cami practically danced onto the field and headed straight for the pitcher's mound.

Over the next two hours I learned several things.

I couldn't hit a ball to save my life.

Cami was scary competitive, and didn't understand the meaning of a friendly match.

And these women had decided I was their friend regardless of how things stood with Weston.

After begging off a third game, I took a seat on the grass in the outfield. My ass was already covered in mud and numb from the cold, so I didn't feel particularly bothered about ruining my clothing at this point. After a moment, Marina wandered over and dropped down beside me.

"Cami warned me you'd find an opportunity to talk."

Marina huffed a laugh, but kept quiet as we watched Cami run the girls through a pitching drill.

"She's really good with them," I observed as Amber cocked her arm and mimed a pitch.

"She wasn't always that good. When the girls were younger and Cami came to visit, before she moved here to help Christian, she acted like the kids were diseased. It was pretty funny, actually. You might have noticed that Cami can be an acquired taste. She had a pretty rough time through college. It wasn't until she moved to Chicago that she started to open up to the idea that she didn't have to fight everything."

"She's so tough. I'd love to be as strong as her."

Marina chuckled. "You are. Just, in a different way. Strength comes in different forms for everyone. It doesn't make you more, or less than, just uniquely you." Her mouth quirked in a small smile.

"If I hadn't known Amber was your daughter, the philosophical shit would be a dead giveaway."

We fell into a comfortable silence as Zara pitched the ball and it landed perfectly in Cami's mit behind home plate. Both girls screamed in excitement as Cami cheered.

"It wasn't real."

Marina stayed silent; her eyes focused on the celebrations across the field.

"The relationship between me and Weston. He saved me from an uncomfortable situation and it kind of snowballed from there."

"He does have a bit of a hero complex," Marina agreed.

"It got out of hand. I mean... I didn't even know who he was at first. And when I found out, I immediately used it for my own benefit."

The story poured out in stops and starts. My proposal and Weston's acceptance. How we deceived friends and family, and how it ultimately came apart.

When I was finished, I felt exhausted.

"Have you ever spoken to anyone about your family?" she asked eventually.

"I complain about them all the time. No one ever listens."

She finally glanced over, a warmth in her eyes that I didn't expect after having aired all my dirty laundry. "I mean, someone professional."

"I'm pretty sure I'd be locked up if someone started digging around in my head," I joked, but she just watched me quietly for another long moment.

"I guess I didn't ever think it was something worth getting into therapy for. Who wants to listen to me whine about my shitty family when there are people out there who really need help?"

"Everyone deserves to feel heard. Whether that's by friends, family, or a professional depends on their circle. Forgive me for saying so, but it sounds like you haven't had a whole lot of people to rely on, and those that were there don't sound like great supports."

"They weren't."

"So what support would you like to see?"

As the temperature dropped and the first snowflakes touched down around us, Marina gently but firmly helped me work through some long-held beliefs that didn't serve who I wanted to be.

She congratulated me on my decision to speak out against Denny Hayes, agreed with Weston's suggestion of no contact... and gently suggested that maybe my sister wasn't the villain I'd made her into over the years.

When we stood and stretched out our cold muscles, my mind raced ahead in a to-do list that scared and elated me.

I was going way out of my comfort zone.

And a part of me knew it was well overdue.

CHAPTER
SEVENTEEN

Gia

A SENSE of déjà vu settled over me as I took my seat between Cami and Ridley at the game the following weekend. The nerves were the same. The crowd was just as loud. But everything was completely different.

The tickets had arrived at my door accompanied by a huge bouquet of flowers and a paint by numbers set along with a note from Weston formally inviting me to the game. After my talk with Marina, I'd wanted to reach out to him immediately, but if I'd learned nothing else from our talk, I knew I had some serious self-improvements to make. So around my filming schedule, I'd found a new manager who came highly recommended, and her first point of business was putting me in touch with the police to add my own report about Denny Hayes.

I'd also asked Marina for the number of a therapist. As easy as it would have been to keep putting my baggage on Marina, it wasn't fair or healthy for our friendship to blur those lines. I had my first appointment with a psychologist who specialized in family trauma after the holidays.

I hadn't directly done anything about my parents yet, but planned on having a conversation in person when I flew down in a couple of weeks. My main goal for the visit was something that terrified me more than anything else on my list.

Asking Blair for forgiveness.

The game started off well, with the Engines winning the coin toss and opting to receive the ball. I cheered along with everyone else as Weston, Christian, and the rest of the offense took the field. Christian caught the snap and passed the ball through to the running back, who managed to break through the defensive line and run the ball ten yards before one of the Greenville Generals' defensive players brought him to the ground.

They set up for their second play, and just before he settled into position, Weston turned around and pointed directly at us.

"He's playing for you," Ridley murmured, her excited energy bubbling out of her in waves.

This time, as Christian took the snap, the running back bolted right, acting as decoy as Christian dumped the ball off to Weston. He caught the pass and broke through the defensive line.

"Oh my god! Yes!" I screamed, jumping to my feet along with half the stadium as Weston outpaced the opposition. For a minute, I thought he would run all the way and score a touchdown himself, but as the Generals players closed in, he tossed the ball back to a wide receiver. Weston disappeared under a mountain of players as his team mate took off down the field and slammed the ball into the ground as he crossed the end zone. The celebration was deafening as Engines fans screamed their approval. It had been difficult for everyone to watch our offense struggle in the last couple of games. I grinned at my friends, expecting to see the same excitement on their faces.

"What?" I asked, noting their silence.

Cami's face was pale, and as I looked back at the field, I noticed a strange hush taking over the stadium. The entire offensive line had huddled around something on the field, and as I craned to see what everyone else had, my stomach dropped as I realized they were standing around the position I'd last seen Weston.

"No." I climbed onto my chair, trying to get high enough to see. Surely he was amongst the players standing around. He was fine. I just had to find him.

Medical staff ran onto the field carrying a stretcher, and my gut churned as I caught sight of long strands of blond hair along the ground in between the players' boots.

"Weston!" Ridley and Cami caught me as I lurched forward, forgetting I was on a chair. I sagged to the floor between them as the players continued to mill around.

After what felt like a lifetime, Weston got to his feet, supported on both sides by his team mates as he cradled his arm close to his chest.

"He's injured his shoulder again," Cami muttered, her voice thick with empathy.

"Let's have a round of applause for number eighty-two, Weston Naylor, folks!" the announcer called as Weston stumbled toward the edge of the field.

The clapping was deafening as I sank into my chair, unsure whether I should go to him or wait here.

"We'll meet them at the hospital. Come on." Cami ushered me out of the suite and didn't let go of my arm until we'd reached her car in the parking lot. "You think you're alright to stand?" she asked, easing her hand away like she expected to have to catch me.

"I'm fine. Just worried about him. Let's go."

The drive to the hospital passed in an overwhelming flood of worry with Cami repeatedly assuring me we would stay until we were sure he was alright. Even if it meant camping out in the hospital all night.

"Marina is taking the girls home and promised to send Ridley in with supplies," she assured me as we navigated the sterile corridors of the hospital. The only bright side so far had been a nurse who recognized me as Weston's girlfriend and pointed us in the right direction. Turned out fame could sometimes come in handy.

After a few more turns, we arrived in a waiting room where we were told we couldn't go any further until we had advice from his attending physician. The nurse invited us to take a seat while we waited, but refused to give us any information about Weston.

"We just want to know if he's all right," I insisted, struggling to contain my anxiety as visions of medical complications turned my stomach. What if he went into surgery and never came out?

"Gia, sit down. Coach Laudner will be able to find out what's happening when he arrives," Cami said, stretching out in one of the plastic chairs lining the wall. I let out an unimpressed humph, but settled in next to her to wait.

"Gia, wake up. He's asking for you."

I jolted awake, wincing as pain shot through my neck from the awkward position I'd fallen asleep in.

"Weston?"

"He's out of surgery and asking to see you. Will you go in?" The dark smudges under Cami's eyes spoke of the hours we'd waited for news of Weston's condition. The waiting room we sat in was filled with the huge bodies of the entire Chicago Engines team spread out over every available surface.

I pushed out of my seat and picked my way through the bodies to where a woman in a white coat stood in the doorway.

"He's in room five, at the end of the hall on the right. He's still a little drowsy, so be patient with him."

I nodded at her and tried to keep myself to a walk as I approached his room.

The astringent scent of antiseptic burned my nostrils as I stepped into Weston's room. The steady beeping of a heart rate monitor was both comforting and unsettling. In the center of the room, Weston lay shirtless beneath the sheets, his shoulder wrapped in layers of bandages. My heart skipped as tired hazel eyes flipped over to me.

"Hey you," I said gently, moving over to the chair set up beside his bed.

"Hey yourself. I wasn't sure you were here."

"Where else would I be?"

He glanced away, but in that moment, a conversation from months ago came back to me. The scene was exactly what he had described last time, only we weren't the people who he had described.

"I'm not her."

"I know."

But still, he wouldn't meet my eye.

It was time for me to be brave and throw my cards on the table.

"I fucked up. Going home for Thanksgiving was a

terrible idea in a whole line of terrible ideas I had over the course of that visit. You tried to be the voice of reason, and instead of listening to you, I treated you like the enemy. It wasn't right, and I regretted it straight away, but I'm stupidly stubborn so it took some time, and friends I don't deserve, to help me see it."

The ghost of a smile flickered over Weston's beautifully serious face, but it was gone a moment later as he turned his head to look at me straight on.

"I'm not going to be able to play football again."

My heart broke for him. After all the work he'd put in to get back on the field for this season, the end of his career had to be a bitter pill to swallow.

"I'm so sorry."

He studied me closely, his eyes flicking over my face like he was searching for a specific reaction. I wasn't sure what he hoped to find.

"I don't know what I'm going to do next."

"Maybe both of us can get a job at Dairy Queen," I suggested, then snorted at the horrified look he gave me.

"Why would you be working there?"

I explained the case against Denny Hayes, and his eyes darkened with anger, despite me glossing over my own experience.

"I knew I didn't like that guy."

"No one does. And now we're going to make sure he can't hurt anyone else."

He was quiet for a few more minutes, chewing over the new information, then he turned his hand over on the bed. I gripped it and smiled as he brought my fist to his mouth for a kiss.

"Whatever happens next, I'd like you to be with me to see it," he said against my knuckles.

"Yes," I whispered.

"You are the best lie I ever told, but I'm going to tell you something and I need you to hear it. This thing we share was never fake. You were mine from the moment I first saw you."

Tears blurred my eyes as I leaned in and pressed a gentle kiss against his lips.

"I want to be yours."

The beeping of his monitor sped up as he tried to heave himself upright, letting out an annoyed grunt as his shoulder hampered his movement.

"All I want is to touch you right now, but I might have to put a pin in my plans until I have two working arms. Unless you want to lock that door and give me a show." He bounced his eyebrows, and I laughed at his antics.

"I think your doctor is going to have to clear you for strenuous activity. But I promise, I'll give you an IOU."

He hummed as he cupped the back of my head, pulling my mouth to his. "I loved redeeming the last one."

"I love you."

We both froze at the admission. It was a truth I'd been holding for a while, but it felt too soon to say it. I had so much work left to do on myself to feel even halfway worthy of calling him my boyfriend.

"I love you too."

"Really?"

"Georgie, you're the most real person I've ever met. You're fun, unpredictable, and more caring than you let anyone see. How could I not love you?"

Tears spilled down my cheeks as I smoothed his hair back and pressed kisses all over his face until he caught my mouth in a scorching kiss.

"As soon as I'm out of this hospital bed, I want to talk to

you about moving in with me. I hate the idea of you staying alone in that apartment building."

"Focus on recovering and then we'll talk about you letting a hurricane like me into your life on a more permanent basis."

He huffed a laugh and settled back against his pillows.

"I can't wait."

CHAPTER
EIGHTEEN

Gia

"I THINK I'm going to be sick," I muttered, breathing in through my nose and blowing the air out through my lips. My stomach crawled as I tapped my fingers against my thigh.

I'd left Weston at home, under the watchful eyes of nurse Amber and nurse Zara who had solemnly sworn they would keep Weston company and ensure he was fed a steady diet of his favorite cookies until I returned. The memory centered me as I double checked the address Weston had gotten from Cian.

After he was released from hospital the week after Christmas, he'd reached out to my sister's hockey player boyfriend and had opened a frank conversation about the toxic household Blair and I had been raised in. I didn't want to know all the details, but when Weston broached the possibility of me meeting with them to make amends, they were surprisingly open to the suggestion.

Which was how I found myself standing out the front of a lovely little villa in Barton Creek, just outside Austin.

I fiddled with my purse strap for a moment before sliding my phone out and shooting off a text.

Georgie: I wish you were here.

Weston: You've got this. No matter how it goes down, you both deserve the closure.

Georgie: I love you

Weston: I love you too. Stop procrastinating.

I choked on a laugh and dropped my phone back in my purse before taking a deep breath and walking up to the front door.

My knock was filled with a confidence I didn't feel, and I immediately worried I'd started off on the wrong foot. Would they think I was there to fight because I'd knocked so hard?

My palms grew damp as I waited for the door to open. Footsteps sounded from inside, and a moment later, the dark-haired man I met at my parent's house appeared.

"I'm going to be honest," Cian said, leaning in the doorway without bothering to let me in. "I was against this little meeting, even after Weston told me a bit about your side of things. You need to know that I love your sister, and if I get even the slightest inkling that you're upsetting her, I'm going to show you the door. Do you understand?"

"Okay, easy there, hotshot. She understands the riot act, now let her in." My sister's voice murmured from somewhere behind his bulk.

Blair looked just the same, and yet completely different as her hockey guard dog let me through the door. Her wild curls hadn't changed. Her glasses were as big as ever, and she wasn't wearing a lick of makeup. But her face glowed with a happiness I'd never seen in her before. One she never would have experienced around our family, or in the house we grew up in.

"You look good," I said, by way of greeting. "Happy."

"I am," she said with a smile, her brow creasing as she cocked her head at me. I wasn't surprised. The last time I'd voluntarily said something nice to her had probably been when we both still played with dolls.

"Do you want to sit on the sofa?"

I glanced around their home and felt like an intruder, so I shook my head and stayed where I was.

"Okay. So I guess we're just going to do this." Blair crossed her arms, bracing for whatever came next. "I have to admit, I was surprised when Weston reached out to us. After Thanksgiving, I thought we'd be disowned."

I swallowed the words *you would be so lucky* and nodded instead.

"A lot has happened recently, and it's caused me to... reevaluate... some of my long-held beliefs and motivations. I owe you an apology for... I don't know. The last decade or so?" My throat tightened as I saw surprise, wariness, and then sadness flicker across my sister's face. A face I'd known for most of my life. One I'd been using against her for far too long.

"I don't even know where we fell apart. When did we stop acting like sisters?"

Blair's eyes were big behind her glasses, and the ingrained, nasty part of me wanted to lash out. To make a snide comment and blow up this uneasy truce. I thought about Weston. About the future I wanted with him, if I was brave enough to do the work on myself and go after it. I deserved better. And that meant honesty.

"I know exactly when it happened. Do you remember

the camping trips Dad used to take you on when we were kids?"

Blair nodded. "Yeah, they were awesome. Some of my best memories were fishing with Dad."

I bit my lip against a snarl. I'd talked this through with Marina the week before, and she'd helped me realize that Blair was just a kid. She wasn't to blame for the actions of adults.

"Do you remember how many times I asked to come along? Wait. Forget that. Do you remember the time Dad said yes?"

Blair frowned. "You never came with us."

Emotion burned through my chest and I blinked hard. What a stupid thing to get upset by.

Be kind, Georgia.

"No," I said, willing my voice to stay even. "I didn't. But there was one time Dad agreed I could come. I was so damn excited. Especially because he was getting out of the house to avoid one of Mom's crash diet moods. You remember the kind: the *lock the fridge and monitor every morsel of food anyone ate because she didn't want to gain weight by osmosis* kind? He told me to go pack a bag while he got the car together."

A tear slipped down my cheek, and I brushed it away with a shaking hand.

"You left. I heard the car start, and I remember thinking I must have lost time and Dad was getting impatient, but when I ran outside, you were already halfway down the street. I still remember the stupid break lights as you turned the corner and disappeared."

"I didn't—" Blair started, but I held up a hand.

"I know. Now, I know. But for a long time, I couldn't separate you and Dad. He was always there to protect you while I was stuck with her. That day was the final straw for me. I figured if I couldn't join them, beat them. So I tried. Everything I could take from you felt like a win, but it always hurt me just as much. You were this smart, friendly person who deserved Dad's love and attention, and I was the one who got left behind. I blamed you for all of it, and for that I'm sorry." I huffed a laugh. "I'm sorry for a lot of things, I guess. I don't expect this to change anything, maybe we're way past that, but I finally found people who showed me I deserve peace, and I'm so tired of carrying this resentment around. So I'm letting it go."

Tears slipped down Blair's cheeks as she stepped forward and wrapped her arms around me.

"I spent years wanting my sister back. That's all I wanted. I'm sorry our parents are such fucked up assholes."

My laugh turned into a sob, and then I was hugging Blair as tightly as she held me as we cried for the people we used to be.

"They really are assholes," I said, hiccupping a watery laugh.

As the tears dried up on both sides, we pulled back and I tried valiantly to fix the damage I'd made to my makeup.

"Ugh, this is what I get for not wearing waterproof mascara."

"You don't need it. You're beautiful without it. You always have been."

I gave her a sad smile. "It was never about the makeup. It was about making sure there was one less thing for Mom to criticize."

She hummed and glanced at Cian, who stood off to the side, watching unobtrusively. Immediately, her eyes warmed, and for the first time, I truly appreciated that my sister had found love.

"I owe you another apology. For Thanksgiving. Weston and I weren't really dating. We've only officially been together a couple of weeks. I was so scared of Mom finding out and ripping me to pieces that I threw you under the bus. I'm a shitty sister, but I promise I'm going to do better from now on."

Blair huffed a laugh and glanced at Cian, who nodded in answer to her unspoken question.

"We were kind of only friends with benefits at that point. I only asked Cian to come along so I wouldn't have to deal with Mom comparing you with your perfect face and athlete boyfriend to me and my... arrangement. She tried to set me up with Scott Ronson a few months ago."

I couldn't suppress the laugh that burst out of me.

"That guy was disgusting."

"You're telling me. So I guess what I'm saying is that we're both dirty rotten liars with the worst kind of parents, and maybe it's time to clean the slate and start fresh."

"I'd love that."

I stayed for a few more hours, catching up on Blair's life and updating her on my own as we navigated this new phase we'd entered. I didn't know if we'd be able to build on what we'd started, or if the foundations were beyond repair and time and distance would cause a greater separation, but as I sat back in my business class seat, courtesy of Weston, I was optimistic that we could create a better life for all of us.

EPILOGUE

12 months later

GEORGIA

"GEORGIE, are you ready to go? We need to—" Weston cut off sharply as he wandered into our walk-in closet to find me in nothing but a lacy thong I'd found when I decided to clean out my shelves.

"I might have distracted myself from packing," I admitted, turning to face him and enjoying the way his eyes dropped to my chest.

"We're catching a later flight," he growled, stalking through the room and scooping me into his arms.

"Did I make us late again?" I asked, grinning unrepentantly as he strode toward our king-sized bed.

"No, but I'm about to." He tossed me in the middle of the mattress, crawling after me with a hungry look in his eye.

"Blair is expecting us there in time for the dress rehearsal."

Weston flicked a glance at the window, then got busy settling between my thighs. "Our flight was delayed by a snow storm. Nothing to be done but wait it out. Now, how about you ride my face?"

I lifted my hips and let him slide the thong down my legs, shivering as he kissed his way from ankle to the crease of my thigh. Without conscious thought, I let my knees drop open and thrust a hand through his hair as he took the invitation and drove his tongue deep into my aching pussy.

He had suggested cutting his hair off after his official retirement from football, but I'd nixed it immediately. He saw things my way as soon as I mentioned how much I enjoyed holding it while he ate me out.

"West," I whined, lifting my hips to meet his tongue as pleasure flooded my system, lighting me up from the inside out.

"What do you need, princess?" he asked, lapping at my clit with firm strokes of his tongue.

"I want you inside me."

He sucked my folds into his mouth, pushing two fingers into my pussy as deep as he could go.

"You want to come on my cock?"

"Yes," I groaned, tugging on his hair until he crawled up over me.

"You want me to fuck you nice and deep?"

"And hard," I said, working his zipper open.

"And hard," he agreed, and pushed his jeans down over his ass. Despite his retirement, Weston had continued to train like he still played professional football, and I was certain that Weston Naylor's ass dot com would still appreciate what he had going on back there. But these days it was only for my viewing pleasure.

I cried out as he hooked his hands behind my knees and pulled me beneath him, fully seating himself in one hard thrust.

"Is this what you want?" he asked, driving into me in powerful strokes that caused sparks to flash across my vision. "God, yes," I cried, digging my nails into his back and groaning as he sank his teeth into my shoulder in retaliation.

"Fuck, you feel so good, princess. Tell me you're close. I want to feel you come all over me."

"I'm close. I'm — yes. There. Please." I babbled incoherently as he thumbed my clit and pushed me into a mind-numbing orgasm.

He rode out my shudders, slowing his pace until I stilled before chasing his own release. When we were finished, he disappeared into the bathroom, returning a moment later with a warm washcloth to clean me up before he began packing both our bags to head to the airport.

"I have a confession to make," he said as we retrieved our bags from the back of the Uber.

"I booked our flight for an hour later than I told you. Just in case."

I wanted to yell at him, but seeing as I'd made us miss every flight we'd taken in the last twelve months, I didn't have the track record to argue with his logic.

"You're lucky I love you," I grumbled half-heartedly. He chuckled and pressed a kiss on my cheek before leading the way into the terminal.

As we waited for our boarding call, Weston's phone pinged with a text.

"Wayne says good luck at the wedding." He huffed a

laugh. "And to make sure you catch the bouquet so Weston makes an honest woman out of you."

Wayne Desmond had turned out to be the last piece to our little found family. He had become a father figure to Weston as he navigated his new career as a sports commentator, introducing him to the who's who of the media and ensuring Weston's transition was as smooth and drama free as possible.

His daughter, Sophie, had made fast friends with Amber and Zara, and the pair had even submitted their own entries for the over-the-fence bakeoffs that Weston and Amber still held.

"I've never met anyone more in love with love. Especially seeing as he doesn't have anyone himself."

"I'm pretty sure he's living vicariously," West murmured as he slipped his phone into his pocket.

Our flight passed uneventfully, and in no time we were pulling up in front of Blair and Cian's house. As I took a step toward the house, Weston caught my hand.

"Wait. Before we go in there, I want to tell you something."

I waited patiently as he tucked one hand in his pocket and squeezed my fingers gently.

"I told you once that I'd always have your back," he started, and I smiled, thinking of how much he'd proven the fact over the last twelve months.

"There was a period there where I don't think I did a very good job of it, but on the other side of it you proved that you're a force of nature. You are more than I could have ever dreamed of in a partner, and I'm so damn lucky to call you mine. I know it isn't the right time, and I know I could have made it more special, but I also know that this might make it just that bit easier to walk through that door.

Georgie, I love you more than I can ever express. Would you marry me?"

He pulled his hand from his pocket, holding out a beautiful emerald and diamond ring set in yellow gold.

"You just had to ask." I gave him a cheeky grin, because what else could I say when the love of my life offered me forever?

He pulled me against him, stroking his tongue along my lips until I opened to him as he slipped the ring onto my finger. Light spilled across us as the front door opened and my sister let out a wolf whistle loud enough to wake the neighbors.

"Get a room or come inside for drinks, you two. It's party time!"

I broke away from Weston with a laugh, noting the genuine look of happiness on my sister's face as she watched us.

"So... after tomorrow, how do you feel about planning another wedding?" I asked, holding up my hand.

"Fuck yes," she cried, bolting down the walk to tackle me in a hug. Her giant dog, Seelie, sat in the doorway, watching us as we slowly made our way back to the house.

My heart felt big enough to burst as Weston placed a possessive hand on my back.

Tomorrow was my sister's wedding day.

I'd just agreed to marry the love of my life.

Shifting Sands had kept me on as a regular character, even after I testified against Denny Hayes and had the pleasure of hearing him sentenced to several decades of imprisonment.

My reality had become everything it had taken me most of my life to realize I deserved.

And I wouldn't change a thing.

***

Thank you so much for reading!

If you loved Gia and Weston's story, please consider leaving a review.

ARE you curious about Gia's sister, Blair, and her hockey hunk? Their story, SLAPSHOT is available now!

Want to spend some more time getting to know Cami Morales? Her book, WILD PITCH is coming soon.

SIGN up for TL's newsletter to find out about new books!

NEXT UP IN the Gridiron Warriors series is Sideline Sweetheart by Michelle Rene

MEET THE GRIDIRON WARRIORS

Protecting Player #73: Portland Settlers
    by KL Donn

Rushing Her: Seattle Westerners
    by E.M. Shue

False Start: Chicago Engines
    by TL Hamilton

Sideline Sweetheart: Greenville Generals
    by Michelle Rene

Flag On The Play: New York Nighthawks
    by Heather Dahlgren

Player #4: San Antonio Rattlers
    by Annelise Reynolds

Kicked in the Heart: Indianapolis Legends
    by L.A. Remenicky

Playing For Keeps: Columbus Jaguars
    by Michelle Savage

Fumbling Forward: Dakota Dragons
    by Kathleen Kelly

The First Down Loses: Charleston Crazed Lunatics
    by Chelle C. Craze

Safe to Love: Salt Lake City Saints
    by Rachelle Stevensen

The Game Plan: Knoxville Kings
    by Janet Berry

Off Sides: Las Vegas Fortune
    by Cedar Rose

Defending Rush: Colorado Cougars
    by Xana Jordan

Quarterback Sneak: Midland Mavericks
    by Haven Rose

Personal Foul: St. Louis Mad Dogs
    by Maria Vickers

Hail Mary: Daytona Devils
    by Quinn Ryder

The End Zone: San Francisco Wolves
    by Tarrah Anders

AUTHOR'S NOTE

What a ride! Thank you for picking up Gia and Weston's book.

While it wasn't lengthy, False Start was a deceptively difficult book to write. Gia's focus issues became my own as I struggled to pull together their love story with Weston sitting off to the side and shrugging at me. "I just love her, ok?"

Starting a story with a character who had previously been portrayed as an antagonist meant that I had to dig into the 'why' of her nastiness. There had to be more of a reason to her treatment of Blair than just being the Anastasia/Drusilla to Blair's Cinderella.

Her undiagnosed ADHD came out pretty early, and the subconscious debate then became to diagnose, or not to diagnose. For those of you who follow me on socials, you may already know that I work in mental health in my day job. Women have a much harder time receiving a diagnosis than men due to gender differences in presentation, as well as social norms that encourage women to develop masks early. The demographic of clientele I work with have often found out their diagnosis later in life, and are grieving for their inner child who struggled with feelings of worthlessness because their neurospicy selves weren't understood or accommodated for.

You may be asking "then why didn't you let Gia have the closure of a diagnosis?" and the answer is simple and twofold.

1. It is easy to build an identity around a diagnosis, and I decided Gia deserved to learn self acceptance and build a positive social network, and

2. The symptoms she presents with can also be seen in those with PTSD, and borderline personality disorder (yes, I'm aware of the updated terminology of this diagnosis, but seeing as I have very strong opinions about the new term, I'm going to continue using the old one)

If just one person can see themselves in Gia, I'll consider this book a success.

The other theme present that I'd like to highlight is sexual assault. This storyline, while only alluded to, can be distressing for some readers, and may bring things up for you. Please take care of your mental health, and if you do wish to speak up about something from your own experience, please reach out to your local supports.

Sexual assault resources
USA - National Sexual Assault Hotline at (800) 656-4673
Australia - 1800RESPECT
UK - **Rape** & Sexual Abuse Support Line 0808 500 222

Finally, if you are reading this after having read Slapshot, then yes, Weston's position was changed. In the final round of edits, I changed him from a fullback to a tight end at the advice of someone who knew a whole lot more about American Football than my little Australian self.

Thank you again for reading this, and hopefully I'll see you soon for Cami's story!!

ALSO BY TJ HAMILTON

M/F Sports Romance

The Perfect Stroke

Split - Kane & Darcy Pt 1

Shatter - Kane & Darcy Pt 2

Shock - Evie & Xavier

Fox Academy

Kicking it with the Winger Oscar & Mia

Austin Aces Hockey Club

Slapshot Cian & Blair

Warrior Sports League

False Start Weston & Gia

Wild Pitch Cami & Gage

M/F Military Romantic Suspense

At All Costs

Target Me

Heal Me

Contemporary RH

The One For Us

The not so secret life of a wish maker

Where in the world (Stand alone in 'The One For Us' universe)

Goldenfire Records

Not With the Band

Zodiac Assassins

The book of Gemini

Paranormal RH

Moon Dust Library/ Silver Springs Library Standalones

Moonlit Alexandrite

Moonlit Alexandrite: Crafty Seductions

Jewels Cafe: Jacinth

The Cursed Coven of Spells Hollow

Warrior Witch (co write with Katherine Isaac)

ACKNOWLEDGMENTS

I would love to say that writing a book is easy.

That I have some kind of beautiful routine where I sit in a calm bubble where the coffee is always hot and the words always flow.

But that is so far from the truth I may have to straighten out of the twisted prawn position I'm sitting in and laugh while adjusting the couch cushion behind my back.

My first thank you has to go to my amazing Alpha reader, Jamie, who has been with me from the start and still puts up with weeks of one or two hundred words, followed by days of panic writing where all the chapters that have been boiling away in my head finally pour out in a manic flood.

I also need to thank Jamie for roping her sister, Dawn into helping this time.

Dawn, thank you so much for your feedback. I genuinely couldn't have made the football scenes half what they became with your careful and considered feedback.

It turns out, a working knowledge of Australian rules and Rugby league football was not a transferable skill when writing American football.

Who knew?

Zainab, as always, your editing gave me confidence in my work that I didn't feel when I submitted the story to you with a "please tell me it doesn't suck".

I can't tell you how much I appreciate my entire support network. You all mean the world to me.

To all the friends who reach out to ask how the writing is going, and what I'm currently working on: I can't tell you what it means to know people are cheering me on when I'm in the aforementioned manic writing states.

To my husband and boys who so generously wander off to play Fortnite so I have space to write, I love you with my whole heart.

And to you, the reader. Thank you for seeing my characters, flaws and all. I hope you found something in here that spoke to you, and that you'll come back to see more of these characters find love as this series progresses.

Until next time, happy reading!

About the Author

TL Hamilton hails from Melbourne, Australia, where she lives with her hubby, two (not so) little boys, and menagerie of animals.

The consummate daydreamer, TL writes all over the romance spectrum from romcom right through to the dark, gritty, hold onto your seats drama. Regardless of the story, you can guarantee you'll find relatable characters and steamy bedroom times between the covers of her books.

Reviews are the life blood of indie authors, so if you read her work and enjoy it, please consider leaving a review in exchange for her everlasting adoration.

Come and join the fun in her reader group on Facebook

www.tlhamiltonauthor.com